CASTAWAYS
Two Short Novels

MASUJI IBUSE

Translated by
Anthony Liman
David Aylward

KODANSHA INTERNATIONAL
Tokyo • New York • London

Publication of these translations was assisted by a grant from The Japan Foundation.

"John Manjirō: A Castaway's Chronicle" was first published by Kawade Shobō in 1937 under the title *John Manjirō hyōryūki*. "A Geisha Remembers" was first published by Bungei Shunjū in 1952 under the title *Oshima no zonnengaki*.

First edition, 1987
First paperback edition, 1993
93 94 95 10 9 8 7 6 5 4 3 2 1

ISBN 4-7700-1744-8

Contents

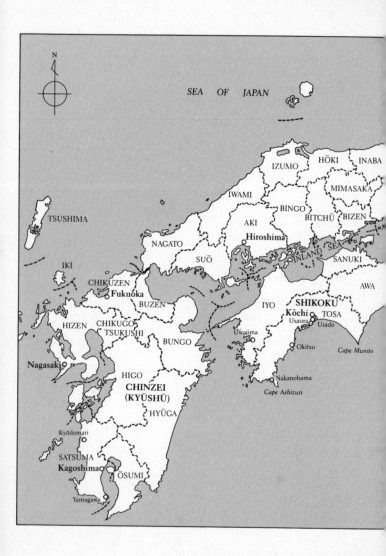

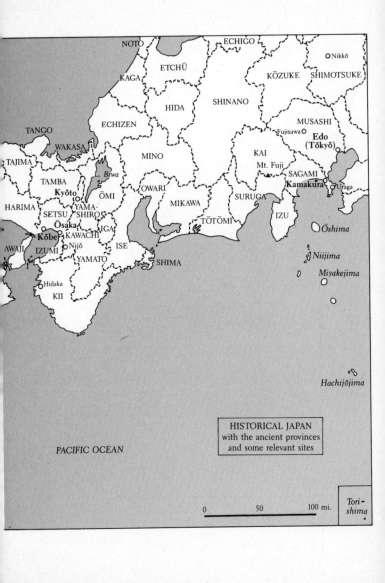

NOTO
ECHIGO
Nikkō
ETCHŪ
KAGA
KŌZUKE   SHIMOTSUKE
HIDA   SHINANO
ECHIZEN   MUSASHI
TANGO   Fujisawa   Edo
WAKASA   (Tōkyō)
TAJIMA   MINO   KAI
TAMBA   Mt. Fuji   SAGAMI
TAJIMA   OWARI   SURUGA   Kamakura   Uraga
L. Biwa   IZU
Kyōto   ŌMI
HARIMA YAMA-   MIKAWA   Ōshima
SETSU   SHIRO   TŌTŌMI
Ōsaka   Niijima
Kōbe KAWACHI IGA
AWAJI   Nijō   ISE   Miyakejima
IZUMI
YAMATO
Hidaka SHIMA

KII

Hachijōjima

PACIFIC OCEAN

HISTORICAL JAPAN
with the ancient provinces
and some relevant sites

0   50   100 mi.

Tori-
shima

Foreword

This volume is in effect a continuation of *Waves*, which appeared from Kodansha in August 1986. The two were originally conceived as one book, to be called *Castaways*, but it was felt that four substantial short novels under the same cover, complete with introductions, notes, and maps, was two too many. Our title finds a particular echo in "John Manjirō: A Castaway's Chronicle," but it describes the plight of characters in the other three stories as well, who become outsiders against their will, cast away by the current rulers of their society.

In addition, there is the reappearing image of the island: those of the Inland Sea that Tomoakira in "Waves" has to hide among, the penal colony of "Isle-on-the-Billows," and in both stories here. Takashima Shū-han in "A Geisha Remembers" is kept under house arrest for his advocacy of coastal defense and "Dutch learning," whose source is the island of Dejima in Nagasaki harbor, sole residence of Europeans in Japan; ironically, it is for trying to defend his island nation from the great world by establishing ties with it that he is himself doomed to isolation. Finally, it is the Island of Birds (Torishima) that saves John Manjirō from a watery grave, and another island, Oahu in Hawaii, that serves him almost literally as a halfway house between Japan and America.

The theme of being cast away and drifting, both in a literal and a figurative sense, provides an important contrast in Ibuse's work to his other favorite theme of rooted, stationary existence. Next to his village stories, whose characters have deeply stable identities, Ibuse seems most interested in the fate of forcefully uprooted people, whether the calamities that beset them are man-made or natural. We might say that he explores the strength of Japanese identity, testing its viability under extreme conditions or in different cultural climates. By extension, the

9

title stands for Ibuse's basic thematic set and his deep sympathy for the peasant underdog or downtrodden everyman—in short, the unknown characters or "failures" of Japanese history.

In addition to the assistance we acknowledged in *Waves*, we would particularly like to thank Miss Aoki Yukiko and The Japan Foundation.

A Geisha Remembers

Introduction

Of all the stereotypes of Japan we have, those of the samurai and the geisha are the strongest. To our gender-conscious culture, they symbolize the twin ideals of the strong man and the beautiful woman, the fierce warrior and the loving sex-goddess. But they come to us at third hand, through centuries of glamorization by the Japanese, then through another century of well-meaning "explanations" to the interested foreigner.

The medieval samurai were often as not treacherous adventurers, greedy and brutal, changing sides more often than their socks. In the later, peaceful centuries of the Tokugawa period (1615–1867), when their ideals had become codified, many became idle wasters encouraged by their legal status to do no work, swaggering bullies who would test their sword edges on unarmed peasants. But the military arts were only a part of samurai endeavor, and many of Japan's greatest statesmen, scholars, and artists have issued from their class, especially from the impoverished lower-ranking samurai. These men were often hard put to make a living and had to sell their swords, marry into wealthy farming and merchant families, or seek humble administrative positions, to survive. The excellent educational system on which Meiji Japan leapfrogged into the modern age was manned by samurai schoolmasters. It was men like the hero of our story, Takashima Shūhan, who helped to pave the way for the Meiji Restoration in the latter part of the Tokugawa period. Without their devotion to learning and their technical expertise, the rapid modernization of Japan would have been unthinkable.

But gaining access to Western science was not easy. Among the many prohibitions the Tokugawa bureaucracy imposed was one against any contact with the West. From the Christian persecution of 1637 to the reopening of the country in 1868, the only Europeans officially allowed into the country were the Dutch, and even they were only permitted to occupy the small, artificially built island of Dejima in Nagasaki, and to take a trip to the capital every two years. The great fear, exacerbated by knowledge of events in China, was that Europeans, assisted by their missionaries, would attempt to annex Japan to their empires. The Japanese people, however, always remained aware of the West not only as a place of exotic customs but as a source of invention, and books on practical subjects like military science, medicine, and mathematics were grudgingly allowed into the country. Groups of scholars sprang up to study these texts, often translated word by word, and they were not without their effect on Japanese life. All the same, suspicion of things Western was so intense that a serious student took his life in his hands—and on occasion lost it, as did some of those mentioned in our story, like Takano Chōei, Watanabe Kazan, and others.

Such were the samurai. Determining the exact nature of the geisha is more complicated. We must first consider the position of women in general—but from an Asian perspective. It should be said that to be a woman in Japan is not seen to be a personal failing. The difference between the sexes is not by Heaven's sanction, but a matter of social rank. Man is not superior because he deserves to be, but because tradition has so decreed it.

To the casual observer, only the prominent surface feature of male dominance stands out. As Kate Millet once observed: "Japan is no place to be a woman," and yet we have to be careful about a sweeping view of this kind. From a historical perspective, Japanese women had at least two major advantages over their Asian sisters. During relatively peaceful centuries like the Heian period it was not considered strange for women to acquire an education, even if it were only by eavesdropping on their brothers' lessons. These were noblewomen, of course, but in Europe in the late Middle Ages, how many women of their station could even read and write?

Secondly, Japanese women were never secluded and so avoided the unfortunate aspects of harem politics. They could go out in the streets, even alone, without inviting remark (or molestation). Even at a time when their lot was hardest and their status lowest—during the strictly regimented Tokugawa period—there were enclaves where freedom from feudal hierarchy was possible.

The pleasure quarters, or red-light districts as we might say, were originally established by the Edo Bakufu to contain all "unruly activities" within a separate, controllable area. They were actually small towns in themselves, with their own firefighters, masseurs, cooks, seamstresses, and musicians. Historically, the geisha are descended not from the prostitutes of these special areas (who could also be of high status), but from the entertainers attached to them.

The pleasure quarters survived until quite recently, and the most famous of them—the Gion of Kyōto, the Yoshiwara of Edo—are remembered in print and picture, film and play. The geisha are all that is left, and they still carry the strong fragrance of an era when townsman and merchant—yes, and samurai—could escape the constant pressure of custom, obligation, and regulation by crossing a moat by a willow tree and finding a little world of his own. The culture of that period would have been colorless indeed without the pleasure quarters: Harunobu, Utamaro and Kiyonaga, Saikaku and Chikamatsu, Kabuki and the puppet theater, shamisen music and kimono design—all had their roots in the "flower and willow world."

We might liken the geisha parties described in the story to the nineteenth-century French salon, or to the bohemian café of our own time. Professional women inhabited a milieu that shut out respectable married women entirely and they understood men's affairs from a detailed, firsthand knowledge.

Ibuse's interest in this story's theme and its protagonist is twofold. First, he is curious about the last years of the Tokugawa shogunate (the Meiji era in the making, as it were), when Japan was still isolationist and Western influence was absorbed only on Japanese terms. The Meiji period itself (1868–1912) has been so well researched by both Japanese and Western historians, and general knowledge of its major events so widespread, that there isn't really much that a writer of historical fiction can "discover" and present to the reader as new. But in "A Geisha Remembers" one has the feeling of being offered a glimpse of a genuinely Japanese society, where the presence of the West is imminent to be sure, yet not so overwhelming as in the later, Meiji years.

Second, Ibuse not only chose a woman protagonist, but entrusted his narration to a female voice: something he had not done before. The work of most modern Japanese writers is remarkable for its detailed investigation of women's experience, and the strength of character (and characterization) shown by their females is the more noticeable when contrasted with the typical weak-willed, neurasthenic hero. Mishima's *After the Banquet* (*Utage no ato*), Tanizaki's *The Makioka Sisters* (*Sasameyuki*), and Kawabata's *Snow Country* (*Yukiguni*) are just three examples that show this trait. If the writer goes a step further and gives a "portrait of a lady" in her own voice, he can make even more play with the stylistic experiment—unfortunately lost in translation—of recreating the highly idiosyncratic manner of feminine speech.

Since Ibuse is famous for his skill in choosing a narrative voice that reveals character with a minimum of outright description, he could not afford to miss such an opportunity. His Oshima speaks in the somewhat formal yet juicy language of downtown Edo, and we have tried to match the color of this lively, everyday idiom in the English version.

While the theme is still within Ibuse's usual range of interest—men and their affairs—the narration and its viewpoint belong to a toughminded, witty, and intelligent woman. The difference between our stereotyped image of the geisha and Oshima's love life as described in this story should be especially revealing to the reader who is interested in seeing the Japanese "at home" instead of acting out cultural myths.

Editor's note: Explanatory notes, arranged according to page number (or chapter, in the case of "John Manjirō"), can be found at the end of the book. Japanese names (except on the title page and jacket) follow the Japanese order—given name last.

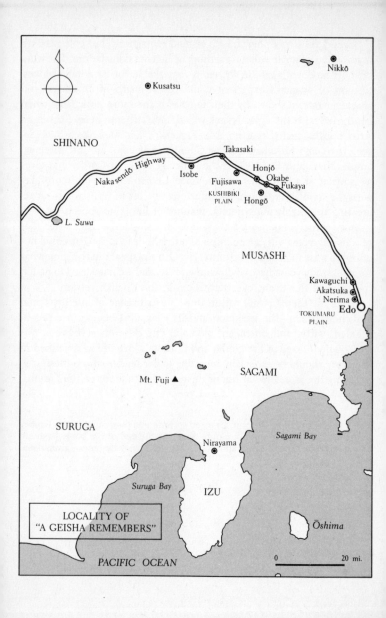

LOCALITY OF
"A GEISHA REMEMBERS"

A Geisha Remembers

The following is a memoir by Oshima, a retired geisha, taken down by some lover of things curious in the fifth year of Meiji [1872], when the old lady was over seventy. In younger days, she had served her calling in the gay quarter of Fukagawa, but in spring of the twelfth year of Tempō [1841], she was caught up in the scandal surrounding Takashima Shūhan. After a first sentence of "severe reprimand," she lost her temper in court and spoke her mind to the presiding official, who re-sentenced her to death a few days later. Luckily for her, a fire near the prison forced the authorities to release her and, in the end, reduce her punishment to a mild form of exile.

Afterward, she went to the Yoshiwara quarter and is said to have been an accomplished dancer and singer, specializing in the Kiyomoto style of ballad.

I was seventeen when I first met Takashima Shūhan at a teahouse in Fukagawa. It was in summertime; Takashima was, oh . . . twenty, or twenty-one. He'd come all the way from Nagasaki on his first visit to Edo, but even to a veteran Fukagawa geisha, he cut a dashing figure. I fell in love at first sight. His companion was Genemon, master of the old Nagasaki Inn in the Hongoku district. They brought a bevy of geisha with them, and a jester Takashima seemed quite taken with.

After the party, Okume, one of my "older sisters," teased me: "You're the one he liked best." I didn't believe it, but what if it were true? I flew to the Temple of the Goddess of Mercy to draw lots for my fortune, and when it promised good luck, I came back on a cloud. And later, when a fortune-teller cast his yarrow stalks for me and mumbled, "Don't you worry. You'll get your heart's desire," I was in seventh heaven. . . . How innocent we were in those days!

After that, I was often summoned to Takashima's parties, but nothing ever happened between us—he just seemed more cheerful when I was around. I felt he'd frown on flirting, even in fun, which made his soirées a little stiff. Gossip said he'd been appointed senior councillor of Nagasaki and commander of artillery at the age of seventeen, responsible both for the city's administration and its coastal defense. Young as he was, with so many people in his charge he couldn't afford to be too free and easy, even on a pleasure trip to Edo. But as time went on, our Edo ways rubbed off on him, and he began to let himself go.

I remember at one party, his jester showed up late without a word of apology and said, "Now, master, guess what I found by the gate. Can't believe my luck—a tobacco pouch worth at least two hundred gold pieces. Made of tooled and gilded leather and tied with a large coral bead, brought from overseas long ago. . . ." Without thinking, Takashima groped in his kimono for his own pouch.

The fool was proud of his trick. He tapped his fan on his forehead and crowed, "Only a joke, master—but I took you in!" Takashima looked down in embarrassment and thought for a moment, then without a word plucked the pouch from his sash and emptied it into a paper handkerchief, before passing it to the jester.

"It's yours now—use it how you like."

His words cast a chill on the party. You see, it was a superbly made pouch, worn for the first time that day. The joker had spotted it through his thin *haori* coat and made up a story *ad lib*. Pure gold fittings, it had, and a netsuke toggle of unicorn ivory. A marvelous piece.

His companion, the innkeeper Genemon, turned to the jester. "Your rudeness has upset Master Takashima. Apologize!" But Takashima stopped him.

"It takes more than a joke to worry me: it's because he's seen through me I'm ashamed." And he gave a man's big laugh. To the fool, he went on, "Don't worry. I was too vain about the gaudy thing. It's ridiculous to be so attached to a trinket. I have to feel if it's there all the time. You hit your mark with that shot—and I deserved it." He laughed again.

By this time, the fool was near dead with embarrassment, so Takashima turned to me. "I want the cheapest kind of shag pouch in Edo. Where can I get one?"

"They have oilpaper ones in Senjugawara," I told him, "for five *mon* apiece."

"Ah. . . ." More to himself than to me, he said, "That sounds like just the thing. I'll use them from now on."

I thought he was joking, but no: the very next time I saw him, he had an oilpaper tobacco pouch. And the time after that. Five years later, when he returned to Edo and asked for me at the teahouse, I saw he had a new one—still made of oilpaper.

"I arrived in Edo only yesterday," he said to please me, "and what do you think I did first thing today? Got another of those natty paper pouches you told me of. My old one fell to pieces, but just try and find a shop in Nagasaki that has them. As soon as I got one, I remembered who told me about them, and here I am." At that party, for the first time in five years, I felt my heart was alive again. . . .

Takashima brought no one with him that time—not even a jester— and I was the only geisha present. When he asked me, I confessed to being very keen on the theater.

"If that's the case," he said, "here's some gate money for you to see the Kabuki," and wrapped a gold coin in paper to pass to me. His kindness made me blush for joy, and before I knew it I was weeping.

"Oh! From now on I'll skip all the plays with my favorite actor. . . . How I'd love to see Nagasaki!" I lost my head, completely mistaking his gesture: "I hear the Great Halberd Festival is worth seeing. I'd go there this minute if I knew you wouldn't scold me."

But Takashima wanted to stop my crying, so to cheer me up he called in four geisha who'd come downstairs with a jester, and before long there was a lively party going. I may have been a bit slow, but I got the point: Takashima took the oilpaper pouch seriously enough, but a passionate affair with someone like me was another matter. And I'd gone chattering on, without a thought in my head. I needn't tell you I never went to Nagasaki—or five miles outside Edo for that matter; nor did I give up my actor, Matsumoto Kōshirō, known as "Kōraiya." In fact, I was more in the theater than out, fighting for his favors with another young geisha. But every year, two months before the Great Halberd Festival,

Genemon, the innkeeper from Hongoku, would drop by with money from Takashima. My advice on the tobacco pouch was that important to him.

Not long afterward, we heard rumors that Takashima was gaining a reputation as an artillery expert. A representative of Lord Egawa Tarō-zaemon had traveled to Nagasaki just to see him work, and came back greatly impressed. Soon more retainers were dispatched to Nagasaki for instruction on firearms. Lord Egawa was then the magistrate of Nirayama Province in Izu, very high in the ranks of the shōgun's vassals, and said to be as strong in virtue as he was wide in knowledge. He was the one who built the famous foundry in Nirayama. Yet his admiration for Takashima, away off in Nagasaki, was wholehearted. I picked up this news from guests at my parties, who would discuss all sorts of subjects, risky ones at times. Some would drop hints that Takashima was following in Ōshio Heihachirō's footsteps, the notorious rebel of 1837. Others said he mightn't carry out Ōshio's violent schemes, but Torii Yōzō of the Bakufu police was saying he would, and plotting to catch him on a false charge. Talk was sometimes very loose, about bad blood between lords Egawa and Torii. Whatever the case, popular opinion of Takashima followed Lord Egawa's, and he was praised as a man of character and a genius in the art of gunnery. Having private means, he was able to get things shipped from Holland: howitzers and *mortieren*—as we called mortars in those days—and *druifkogel* shells. He was a master of all methods of loading and firing, knew how to make gunpowder and which kind exploded best on impact, as well as how to maneuver foot soldiers. It was only natural, in later days, for men of talent from all over the country to gather at his gate. After Lord Egawa, Sakuma Shōzan of the Sanada clan in Shinano, Chief Treasurer Kawaji Saemon, Junior Councillor Honda of Etchū, the Sendai clan's Ōtsuki Bankei, and many other notable scholars became pupils of his. But all this came after his artillery demonstration on the plain of Tokumaru in Bushū, held in the twelfth year of Tempō.

It was just before then, in the Twelfth Month of the previous year, that I heard from Genemon that Takashima was coming to Edo again, after a long absence. The visit had been proposed by Lord Egawa to Senior Councillor Mizuno, who after approving it had sent orders to the chief magistrate of Nagasaki. The orders went, in part: "Commander

Takashima is to present himself and his assistants in Edo with all the new Western-style artillery in his possession, including *mortieren*, howitzers, field guns, and small arms."

Takashima, his eldest son Asagorō, and an entourage of students left Nagasaki in the latter part of the First Month the following year and reached Edo without incident at the beginning of the Third Month. As he was making his journey by official order of the Bakufu, I asked Genemon to let me play the role of maid at his inn, the Nagasaki, and welcome Takashima in style by the gate. Seeing him after such a long while, I didn't think he looked a bit like one of our Edo dandies any more: his black lacquered straw hat had a diamond emblem painted on it, the same crest as on his tight-sleeved *haori*. The two swords thrust in his sash—a long one and a short one—gave him a military bearing. His leggings were of elegant cotton print from Siam, his socks of soft tanned leather, while his sandals were woven from dark blue cord. I was offering him a basin of hot water to wash his feet, when he noticed me.

"Ah, the girl of the oilpaper tobacco pouch!" he said fondly, making me blush, though I was past the age for that sort of thing.

"It's a pleasure to welcome you, sir," I whispered, and kept staring down at his feet.

We put Takashima and his son Asagorō upstairs, his retinue on the ground floor. The crowd of pupils who had accompanied him from Nagasaki had to go elsewhere. Genemon was so pleased at his guest's arrival in state—on an official mission, no less—he put a sign up in the entranceway: "Master Takashima Shūhan's Honorable Hostel" and draped a curtain with his family crest around it. But at Takashima's stern insistence, he had to take it all down.

Poor Genemon shook his head at this: "I'll never understand him." He served nothing but the finest fare, all personally selected, but his guest would only look at plain soup and one kind of vegetable.

The innkeeper was puzzled. "Master Takashima's changed," he told me. "Always very fussy about his food, he was. Only rare, out-of-the-way delicacies would please him, and the saké had to be special reserve. The last time he was in Edo, I strained every nerve to give him the best, but he only made faces. What could I do but take him to the finest gourmet restaurant in town? We had sautéed baby bream and he called it delicious, but after one mouthful of fried ginger, he spat it out." It turned out to be fried in the same oil as the fish, and Takashima's delicate palate detected its flavor on the ginger.

"And now look," grumbled our host, "—'Take that sign down!' he says.... You'd think he was in hiding. Eats nothing but plain food—won't even touch the first bonito of the season."

To my eyes, too, Takashima had grown austere in his ways. One thing did please Genemon, however. "Those cotton leggings show there's some of the old dandy left. What'd you think of that indigo color? A nice touch."

I listened eagerly for Takashima's handclap, but when it came, the innkeeper and his wife would be ahead of me, falling over each other to be first up the stairs. Once when I was waiting for my chance, someone came to the gate, and I went out to see a samurai in formal dress standing there.

"Is the honorable Takashima Shūhan present?" he said, and when I answered, "Yes, he is. The gentleman just arrived today," he said, "Please convey the greetings of the magistrate of Nirayama in Izu, Egawa Tarō-zaemon. Lord Egawa regrets disturbing him after his long journey, but wishes to speak to him." He had a high-bridged nose and large, round—really enormous eyes, bigger than his mouth, you would have been surprised how big they were—and this was the Lord Egawa they talked about so much!

When I took his message to Takashima, a look of keen pleasure came to his face. "Lord Egawa? What a surprise—I must go and see him." And adjusting his formal clothes he went out to show the guest upstairs in person.

Although I was only playing the part of a maid, Genemon thought I meant something to Takashima, so he often talked about what went on upstairs. Lord Egawa had come, as agreed, to help Takashima prepare a rehearsal of the cannon display and round up enough men for his military review.

Through Lord Egawa's good offices, the shortage of men was made up in four or five days, till they had a total of 123. There was one unpleasant incident, though, for me as well as Takashima. He had just left on his way to Bushū—his lodging at Akatsuka village was called the Pine and Moon Temple—to drill his troops, you know, when a trio of scruffy-looking samurai pushed their way up to his room. I was there, on the point of taking some of his personal things downstairs, when they were snatched from my hand.

"What—what are you doing?" I yelled. "That's Master Takashima's!"

"We'll deliver it for you," one of them said. "But it ain't packed right. Should be done up proper." He loosened the string right in front of me, spread the oilpaper wrapping, and began to inspect it. It was just books and writing materials.

"Stop it!" I said, and trying to get their names, "Who are you, anyway?"

One of them grabbed me. "Shut up, you. We're here on the police chief's business. We're taking this stuff to Commander Takashima." I didn't believe a word of it!

Of course, the inspectors had the right to open people's baggage, but it made me hopping mad. Takashima had just been summoned to Edo by no less a personage than Senior Councillor Mizuno, and was made a personal retainer of the Bakufu by one-generation appointment to a suitable post in the city administration. Why, he was practically one of the shōgun's own vassals.

So I screamed at them again, "Lord Takashima is a samurai of the Bakufu! Police or not, you should show him some respect."

"Samurai nothing. He's only a footman. Who're *you*?"

"I . . . I am the maidservant of this inn."

"A maid?—well, you'd better stay out of this."

"Fire!" I yelled, at the top of my voice. "Help, somebody. We're on fire!" I was able to slip out of their hands and grab the ledger one was reading before a rain of kicks and punches knocked me out.

I didn't see what happened next, but Genemon told me later the whole fire brigade arrived, with reinforcements. Gallant spirits all, they gave the three spies a sound thrashing before throwing them into the street. . . . But it worked out badly: especially for me, as the one who defied them first.

You see, the three actually were agents of the police chief, sent by the Bakufu artillery officers Inoue Sadayū and Tatsuke Shirōbei. Their ugly behavior was only meant as a warning, but after that free-for-all, when the firemen came to my rescue and trounced them, the anger

23

of Takashima's enemies was roused to white heat. Inoue and Tatsuke viewed the upstart from far-off Nagasaki, with his newfangled weapons and disciplined troops, as a threat to their own positions in the Bakufu. Added to which, Police Chief Torii Yōzō was the archenemy of his patron Lord Egawa. This was the man who had so misread Senior Councillor Mizuno's well-meant political objectives, and whose agents—they were little more than street thugs, really—were pestering the common people of Edo. It could only be to discredit Lord Egawa that he was ferreting out lapses on his protégé's part. It was Torii who threw Takano Chōei and Watanabe Kazan—the famous scholars of "Dutch learning," as foreign studies were called—in jail, and was responsible for their untimely deaths. I met Master Kazan myself one time: he came to my Fukagawa teahouse with some scholar from Mito, and after I'd served saké he sketched an orchid, which is the same character as "Dutch," on a white fan and added a matching verse while I sat beside him. He was a thin man with narrow, intense eyes set in a puffy face, and he seemed to me a straightforward, upright gentleman.... At any rate, everyone in Edo detested Torii, and I learned from Genemon why he had a grudge against Lord Egawa.

"It was the year before last," he said, "in April or May. On the orders of Senior Councillor Mizuno, Torii Yōzō—at that time a secret agent of the Bakufu—was sent on an inspection tour along the coast of the Bōsō and Izu peninsulas and into Sagami Province. Lord Egawa was his deputy. He took his duties so seriously that, on the advice of Watanabe Kazan, he asked the famous mathematician Dr. Uchida to survey the seacoast there, to get a better idea of its weak and strong points. Well, at last they set out, Torii acting very high-hat and ordering the other man about when he really hadn't a clue about coastal defense. He'd counter any arguments with some cockeyed theory of a 'divine wind' that'd send invaders packing. Lord Egawa got sick and tired of it finally, and cut Torii down to size—made the man lose face before a roomful of his followers—and Torii's hated him ever since, doing his best to slander him to Lord Mizuno." It was Lord Egawa's dislike of such controversy that led him to retire to Nirayama, and he had remained there in seclusion until the time I'm speaking of, when he came up to see Takashima.

As soon as Takashima arrived in Edo, his big bombards were the talk of the town, and Torii must have been eating his heart out. Everybody had heard of his Western-style troops, and was dying to see them in action: from the Bakufu's highest officials to the lords of the realm and their retainers, whether they were in with the Tokugawas or not, no one talked of anything else. Hearing a geisha speak of "artillery" and "coastal defense" will make you laugh, I know, but feeling rather close to the star of the day, I was swept up in the excitement before his arrival. My interest in the planned cannonade was personal; every other day I went and prayed to the Goddess of Mercy for its success, and who should I run into one day by the temple gate but Genemon. He too was praying for our friend's triumph, and on the way home I asked him to escort me to the show.

"That's no problem," he said, "I'll take you along. I want to use my spyglass on the big day, too. But I'm a little worried," he confided. "It shouldn't happen—hardly a chance in a thousand—but the powder may not catch. Keep your fingers crossed."

"The bigger the boom the better, then?" I asked, but he laughed: "That's just what an amateur would say."

Finally the day came, the ninth of the Fifth Month. The cannonade and drill were to be held on Tokumaru Plain near Nerima village, six or seven miles from Edo Castle. Shortly after midnight the day before, I set off with the innkeeper, his wife, and five stalwarts of the neighborhood fire brigade. They carried our lunches wrapped in a large cloth, Genemon kept his spyglass in a rolled cummerbund slung over his shoulder, while Mrs. Genemon and I just had parasols. The half-moon had disappeared, but a starry sky lit the road ahead, and we could easily tell the fields planted with rice shoots from those with wheat stubble. A group of half a dozen young people overtook us on the way and I heard them chaffing one poor fellow:

"Stuffing cotton in your ears already? Shaking in your shoes before you've even heard the cannon fire—what a baby!" Our pace was slow enough to let any number of strangers by us, but I could tell from their conversation they were all going to the display.

"The *bommen* shell's the most popular," I heard one say knowingly, and another, "The shell I go for is the grenade. It blows up with plenty

25

of punch. . . ." None of them had ever seen these weapons, you understand, but they were carrying on as if they'd been Kabuki actors or Sumo wrestlers.

"I just made up a rhyme—want to hear it?" said the innkeeper, but his wife told him to behave.

We reached Nerima village before dawn. As we passed through the Shimonojuku district, a mounted samurai called out:

"If you've come to watch the cannonade, keep well back. Don't go near the pavilions. That's an order!"

The Shimonojuku road was packed with high-ranking samurai, coming and going with an air of self-importance. When I asked about it later, I was told that all officials and noblemen, retainers and two-sworded men who wanted to view the display had to line up in Shimonojuku and report to the marshals. That's why we saw so many bigwigs. I had a good look at one old warrior, who stepped out of his sedan chair to admire the starlit sky and slowly tuck a long sword into his sash. Others had attendants with lances, and sometimes footmen to hold their horses steady while they dismounted and paid their respects.

After we'd gone by, Genemon said gleefully, "Isn't it wonderful! Master Takashima's rounded up the lords of every manor in the land on this one village green."

We called at a farmhouse in the woods and, after catching our breath on the porch, ate our morning snack before the sun came up. The farmer's wife, who was the elder sister of one of our firemen, was a great help to us, lending us some round straw mats to sit on, and describing the lie of the land. We set off as the sky brightened and, from what she'd told us, chose a fine clear view of Tokumaru Plain; there we laid our mats and settled down for a snooze. Leaning against a yew tree back-to-back with the innkeeper's wife, I slept as soundly as if she were a nice warm bolster. I could take catnaps in those days as easily as I do now. It wasn't until the sun came out that I woke up.

On three sides of us, people were swarming like ants. Takashima's little army had just arrived, and the whole line marched past in step, a brave sight. I was straining my eyes to see them when Genemon's wife kindly offered me the spyglass. I was amazed at how close everything looked. Takashima and his son Asagorō were all in black, with narrow-sleeved

26

jackets and breeches, and high-crowned hats like courtiers; they wore gaiters with straw sandals, two swords, and carried batons of command. The soldiers were likewise in black, from their flat helmets and short jackets to their breeches and gaiters; they had blue *tabi* on their feet as well as sandals, and a narrow belt over their sashes to hang powder cases and other gear from. They each carried one sword and had a light, nimble look about them. Takashima looked cool and composed.

To our right, a line of banners with a design of red and white bands had been set up. These were to mark the range of fire: the distant ones were for a thousand yards, the closer ones for five hundred. In the far right-hand corner were several makeshift huts with curtains, one of them quite large. Others had been set up in the westernmost corner for the troops. Away over in the left-hand corner was a battery of cannon and, beside them, an array of lances and small arms; here, all the dignitaries were taking their seats in curtained little pavilions. Their horses were tied in the grove nearby. I gave the spyglass back to Mrs. Genemon. We then heard a low whisper of "Programs here, anyone for programs?" behind us. An unsavory-looking character of about forty stood there, the sleeves of his thin cotton garment tucked up to show tattoos on each upper arm of swords with black snakes coiling around them—the fire-god symbol, I suppose. He pulled out a sheet of paper folded double:

"This gives the details of today's demonstration."

"How much is it?" Genemon asked, and the tattooed man said, "Normally one gold piece, but for you, half. Only one left."

After Genemon had paid, he asked, "Where did you get this agenda?" but Tattoos only laughed in a sneering kind of way.

"Got your information from some musketeer, did you?" Genemon pursued, but the fellow just snickered again and slunk off, pulling another folded sheet from his tunic.

To this day I can remember what was written on the program. I later learned the source of the information was a man named Honjō Moheiji. Nagasaki-born, he was a notorious criminal forced into hiding to escape punishment for his many crimes; kept on the run from place to place, he had eventually gone to ground in Edo, where Torii Yōzō had fished him out of the gutter and made him a plainclothesman. He'd gone back home on Torii's orders to shadow Takashima and cook up a thicker brew of filthy lies for his master. It was this man who spread the rumor that Takashima gave out the leaflets himself. Of course, we learned all this later, and Genemon was unaware of the sinister implications when he bought one, which read like this:

> Commander Takashima Shūhan's troop drill and cannonade, held before distinguished observers on Tokumaru Plain, will take place in this order:
>> A display of accurate shooting at a target from a thousand yards with *bommen* shells fired horizontally from a *mortier*:
>>> –First by Commander Takashima Shūhan;
>>> –Second by Takashima Asagorō;
>>> –Third by Commander Takashima Shūhan.
>> A display of accurate shooting at the same target with *brandkogel* incendiary shells fired from a *mortier*:
>>> –Fourth by Takashima Asagorō;
>>> –Fifth by Commander Takashima Shūhan.
>> A display of accurate shooting at the same target with grenade shells fired laterally from a howitzer:
>>> –Sixth by Takashima Asagorō.

In the seventh and following places were listed the various squads firing salutes with field guns, rifles, and so forth.

The artillery demonstration opened with a signal from a conch shell. Everything was done according to the order on the program. The first round, a *bommen* shell, burst out of the *mortier*'s muzzle with an ear-splitting roar, moving too fast to be seen. Genemon held his breath and peered through the spyglass.

"God—it's incredible. Buried itself in the ground. Amazing!"

My mouth was dry, I can tell you. But the *bommen* had fallen to the right of its mark, seventy yards over. Mrs. Genemon watched the second shot through the spyglass. This one was between forty to fifty yards too long. I was watching myself when the third shell sailed a hundred yards over before burrowing deep into the ground. The crater it made was well past the flag marker. My! what a spectacle—the boom of the cannon, the clouds of smoke—it was enough to make your eyes pop out.

For the next round, with the *brandkogel* shells, one of the firemen was given the glass. "Hey! It's spitting fire," was his comment. "That shell's a real terror!"

It went a hundred and eighty yards or so into the meadow beyond the first line of flag markers. The glass was passed to a second fireman, and from then on to each of us by turns, so that everyone got a look at one round. The grenade fired by the howitzer didn't go too well. It fell into a river about two hundred and fifty yards beyond the target. The *druifkogel* shell was defective and exploded in the air six or seven hundred yards ahead of us. The others were all successful. In the troop drill and rifle salute, the men fired standing in line, turning "right face" or "about face" and back to the first position, attached swords to the ends of their barrels to charge in line, and did all sorts of interesting things, every man keeping in step—a wonderful sight. Takashima gave his orders in Dutch, which I couldn't follow at all, but I was happy enough to sit there wide-eyed and take in the show.

Takashima's military demonstration was a thirty-day wonder. All Edo raved about his amazing skill at gunnery, and when he left Nerima village to return to the capital, the main street of the Hongoku district was lined with curious crowds. Takashima was again staying at Genemon's inn, and both the host and his wife held their heads high as we walked out to the main street to welcome Takashima.

"Congratulations, Master Takashima! It was a truly wonderful spectacle...." The innkeeper got all choked up, with tears of joy running down his cheeks. Mrs. Genemon and I cried, too; we didn't care who saw it, we were so happy.

All sorts of visitors turned up to offer their congratulations. The inn was buzzing with guests, and the three of us were run off our feet showing them in and out. To handle the flood of well-wishers more easily, Takashima moved downstairs. Genemon stayed out in the hall to welcome guests as they arrived, and my job was to conduct them to Takashima, while Mrs. Genemon and the maid Okane stationed themselves inside his rooms to lay out cushions and serve tea. To this day, I remember the very first to congratulate him was Lord Egawa Tarō-zaemon. This was when he was still a high-ranking Bakufu official and universally respected for his wisdom, generosity, and courage.... I can still see his big eyes and high-bridged nose. His attendants carried a basin with a huge sea bream in it as a token of appreciation. Later on, Genemon prepared it with his own hands, but, my, was it big!—two feet long and fresh as they come.

"Lord Egawa must have ordered this from a fisherman beforehand. A monster. The kind that only comes from one place—the harbor of Kanazawa, in Musashi Province." Taking up his kitchen knife, he seemed to be talking to the fish. "Sea bream's no good any smaller." And he began to scale it, in high spirits. Still, it was hard to hook a bream of that size, even in Kanazawa Bay. Lord Egawa must have bought it from a fisherman and kept it in a live-storage well on the seacoast near his mansion in Shiba.

After Lord Egawa, his second visitor was Suzuki Shunzan, a noted scholar of Dutch medicine. Next came a party of three: Takano Chōei, Ozeki Sanei, and Hatai Zenryō. Along with Suzuki, these men were part of the "uptown school" of Dutch scholars who had gathered around Watanabe Kazan. I'd only encountered Dr. Watanabe once before, at the teahouse in Fukagawa, but Genemon had met him a number of times.

"We'll be seeing Watanabe Kazan presently," he told me. "When the whole uptown school shows up, their boss won't be far behind."

We waited expectantly, but after the uptown scholars left, the painter Tsubaki Chinzan came in Dr. Watanabe's place, only to drop off his calling card in the hall before returning. This suited Genemon, for as long as famous names came to his inn he could hold his head up, even if the neighbors didn't see them.

Aside from the uptown group, Itō Gemboku of the "downtown school" came to pay his respects. After him, mentioning only the most important, came representatives from justices Togawa and Taguchi of the Nagasaki magistracy, and from Chief Interpreter Kōjiro of Nagasaki; Sakuma Shōzan of the Sanada clan of Shinshū came in person, as well as Chief Treasurer Kawaji Saemon, Ōtsuki Bankei of the Sendai clan, Junior Councillor Honda of Etchū, Master Ikebe of the house of Hosokawa, and masters Nakanishi and Misawa of the house of Togawa. There were many others. Quite a few were implicated later when Takashima was thrown in prison on false charges, and terrible things happened to them. The samurai were locked up or severely reprimanded;

Justice Taguchi of Nagasaki, the governor of Kaga, who had sent his representative, was placed under house arrest; Izawa, governor of Mimasaka, was "excused from further duties"; and Justice Togawa was shut up in his house, too. Of the three interpreters at Nagasaki who had sent messengers, one was to bé beheaded and have his head displayed, but since he "dutifully returned three times when fire broke out in the shadow of the jail," his punishment was reduced to light banishment outside the twenty-five-mile vicinity of Edo; another was to be crucified, but returned twice when fire broke out near the jail and was sentenced to medium banishment; as was the third, who originally received the same sentence as the first. Aside from their connection with Takashima, Watanabe Kazan and his uptown disciples Takano and Ozeki made the further mistake of meddling with government policy, and met with cruel ends. As I said, this was all the work of Torii Yōzō and his henchmen.

Torii was then Edo's chief of police, with a huge income of three thousand *koku* of rice. We used to call the period of Senior Councillor Mizuno's reform regime the "rain of edicts," because one followed another with hardly any breathing space. Eager to curry favor, Torii always took the edicts a few steps further, plaguing the whole city of Edo like some self-appointed Buddha. Hiding behind Lord Mizuno's power and authority, he had the gall to unleash his spies on the feudal lords of the whole country to inform him of the slightest treasonable activity, and even the shōgun's cousin, Lord Tokugawa of Mito, couldn't do much but look on and be a fool in wise man's clothing. My guests had all kinds of stories to tell and I listened even to their riskier yarns; they seemed to be of one mind about Torii's ways: this monster must have "flying ears and stretching eyes." The Confucian proverb, "a despot is deadlier than a tiger," was often quoted to the discredit of his policies.

I must have told you before, but Torii's right-hand man was an artillery officer employed by the Bakufu, one Inoue Sadayū. This Inoue had a servant, a good-for-nothing called Moheiji—remember the man behind the programs at the cannon display? For what other reason than petty jealousy would these two have tried to smear Takashima's name? The success of his military show had not only brought official commendation from the shōgun himself, but a gift of two hundred silver coins. He had also been directed to present one *mortier* and one howitzer to the Bakufu. Hearing about this, Inoue must have felt his own position as a commander of artillery was being undermined, and to get his own back on Takashima he sent a long exposé to the Bakufu denouncing him. The gist of it was that Takashima's guns were children's toys without any practical use, while the government's secret weapon, a bombard called the "tiger cub," was far more powerful than any of his *mortieren*. His own fireballs had ten times the explosive force of Takashima's incendiary shells. There was a great deal more, on and on, in the same vein.

Lord Egawa was absolutely incensed at this, and publicly refuted Inoue's statement. He said, in effect, that Takashima's ordnance far outstripped the Bakufu's, and when (he wanted to know) had Inoue or his ilk ever fired an actual shell from the Bakufu's secret weapon? Leaders of the nation shouldn't spout empty theories. For all the Bakufu's respect for tradition, weren't its cannon simply old-fashioned models of a type originally from the West? There was no need to be so sentimental about these ancient fieldpieces. What's more, to save Takashima any further trouble, he, Egawa, would take his part in any debate. Or if there were any willing to put his skill in traditional gunnery to the test, he, Egawa, was ready to meet him in the field. Unworthy as he was, no devotee of "the Japanese way" in old-time cannonry would make him give an inch.

These were impressive words, and it took a load off our minds to hear them.

Still, for the Bakufu not to make some criticism of Western methods would weaken its authority. An order came down from the Senior Council; I heard the story many times from Genemon, and I know it by heart even now:

> To Commander Takashima Shūhan, greetings. Concerning the teaching of secret techniques in gunnery: these were to be transmitted to one chosen devotee among the shōgun's immediate vassals, and not revealed at random to members of the various feudal clans. However, at this point there is no objection to giving such instructions as you may wish, providing outlandish headgear or Western-style uniforms are not worn. Furthermore, instead of "Western-style gunnery," the phrase "Takashima-style" is to be used. Lastly, in gunnery or rifle drill, orders may not be given in the Dutch language.

This was in no sense an accusation. In fact it had been issued by Senior Councillor Mizuno at Lord Egawa's suggestion. The "chosen devotee" mentioned in the order was of course Egawa—the only one among the shōgun's retainers skilled in artillery, having received three months' basic training in gunnery from Takashima. In between those lessons, Takashima would drop into the Nagasaki to relax and have a bowl of tea with Genemon. I was in my prime, and my feelings for Takashima had deepened from puppy love into a *grande passion*: throughout those three months I forgot my geisha business and haunted the inn, waiting for my hero to show up. To be honest, there wasn't any kind of liaison worth mentioning between us, but the innkeeper and his wife were convinced, from my way of behaving, that there was. Mrs. Genemon would tease me: "You're looking ripe with love these days, Oshima—there's no doubt about what's going on!" With Genemon it was different: his admiration was so heartfelt he couldn't joke about his idol, though I sometimes wished he would. I just couldn't hide my happiness! When Takashima was there, my heart would pound even taking the tea things up to his rooms. At all the parties I've been to since I was a child, I don't remember my heart thrilling even once as it did then, during those wonderful three months. When Takashima was in good spirits, he would call me his "young seedling seller" and, at other times, simply "Oshima." "The seedling-seller geisha" was my *nom de guerre*. I was called this by my patrons for my constant singing of "The Seedling Seller," a popular *chobokure* ballad of the day. As Lord Mizuno's regime grew stricter, all sorts of commodities disappeared from the streets of Edo like lights being blown out, and people voiced their woes in street ballads:

A seedling, a seed,
Anyone for a seed?
No fresh food to eat,
No eggplant or beans,
Cucumbers, or greens.

Can't powder your nose,
Can't go blossom viewing
Or see puppet shows.

33

Not allowed ballads,
Not even a song. . . .

That's how "The Seedling Seller" went. We sang it in low voices, in case informers were listening.

One evening, while Takashima was staying at the Nagasaki, I decided to stake all on one throw and held my sleeve up to my face, pretending to sniffle while I laid out his sleeping mats. I say "pretending," but before long I was crying real tears! I stopped after a while, realizing that too much of it would defeat my purpose. Stealing a glance at Takashima, I found he wasn't responding—he only looked puzzled at the whole thing. Seeing it was now or never, I went on with the charade of "quarreling with my lover" and, pouting, traced circles on his quilt with my fingertip. My only reward was an embarrassed smile. I wasn't expecting that from a veteran of the pleasure quarters, and I started crying again, from chagrin.

What could I do after that but mumble "Good night" and withdraw? I even forgot to set up his mosquito net.

After I'd turned in myself, I thought about the embarrassed look on Takashima's face, and wondered about its possible meaning. It seemed to be saying, "Act your age. What game are you playing?" Or was it "I haven't time for this. I'll be busy with gunnery instruction tomorrow." Or it might be "A strange twist to our friendship, after all this time!" I turned over the three choices in my mind, wondering which was right, till I fixed on the last. It was nearly dawn before I got to sleep.

That morning I rose late, feeling shy about going up to Takashima's room, but my veteran geisha's spirit sustained me. I clattered gamely up the stairs and called outside his door: "Good morning! Are you up?"

"Ah! Is that my seedling seller?" came the cheerful answer.

When I opened the sliding door, I found him wide awake before a mirror set in one corner of the room, shaving his crown. Hot water had already been poured into a red lacquer washbasin. I briskly slid a cupboard door open as if nothing had happened, and folded away the mosquito net. It was a morning early in the Ninth Month during the storm season; the night before had been sticky, and a clammy, hothouse wind was blowing. While I was rolling up his sleeping mats, I checked the lower one for wrinkles, to see if he had slept restlessly. If I saw any signs of a sleepless night, I could assume my crying and playing at lovers' quarrels had affected him after all, couldn't I? But there were no such signs; what's more, his pillow was neat as a pin. I was piqued, though I tried not to show it, and got a little fresh with him.

"Why don't I do your hair for you?"

"No, it's all right," he said, looking outside. "See how fast the clouds are moving today."

When our host came in to relate the morning's gossip, he told us a government spy had been seen lurking by the pantry door. In those days, Edo was swarming with these spies, who came around to inspect inn and restaurant rubbish dumps. If they found the remains of any vegetable, fish, or fowl that was the first of its season and considered a luxury, you'd be told you were breaking the law and closely questioned. According to the new regulations, frugality was compulsory: townsmen could wear nothing but cotton; women were forbidden to wear gauze, twill, satin, or crepe—to say nothing of silver and gold hair ornaments; and no food could be bought or sold ahead of season. The one who gave these "inspectors" their orders was none other than Torii Yōzō. In his capacity as "investigator of arson and burglary," Torii put police on every street corner and used spies as his "fingertips," rummaging through trash heaps and loitering by kitchen doors. No one was safe: they'd look in fish vendors' wooden buckets and might even stop a woman on the street to see if her underwear was silk or cotton—down to her loincloth! Can you believe they carried scissors openly? And if your sleeves were lined with silk, they'd out with the scissors and say, quite nonchalantly, "Those sleeves need a little trimming, don't they? If madam won't do it herself, we'll help her," and cut them off.

There were even prohibitions on hairdos: if we went out to a play with our hair done too elaborately, we might be stopped and given a grilling. If we'd hired a hairdresser, so much the worse; it was handcuffs, no less. Every type of entertainment, from Edo's three Kabuki companies to "drop curtain" vaudeville and puppet shows, was lumped together and moved to seedy inns behind the pleasure quarter of Asakusa. Whether such measures were right or wrong, Edo townsfolk knew that Torii Yōzō—the toady—would squeeze us all to death to gain favor with those

35

above him; we knew that whatever he did would naturally work against us.

Torii was a know-nothing who loathed anything new—looked on it as you would a poisonous snake. Men like Takashima and Lord Egawa were his bêtes noires, since they were similar in spirit to the uptown scholars; their mere existence made Torii and his gang see red, want to stamp them out. The Izu coastal defense affair added fuel to their hatred, for Lord Egawa had heaped shame on their master. Inoue Sadayū, Torii's pet cannon-buster, was eaten up with jealousy of Takashima's new techniques. And Takashima and Lord Egawa were such chums it was no wonder master and man were out to get them. Torii's estates brought him in three thousand *koku* of rice a year, while Inoue took in nearly nine hundred. Torii had status among the samurai, too, for although born to the scholarly family Hayashi, who made their living teaching, as second son he was entrusted to the Toriis as their son-in-law; to impress his foster family he climbed higher and higher till he rivaled the Buddha himself. Yes, they said it was being henpecked by his rich wife that made him so ambitious, and a man like that in an official position is always a disaster; the ones who suffered for it, of course, were the townspeople of Edo, who could do nothing but cry themselves to sleep. Depending on how the wind was blowing, even those who'd done him favors might have the mat pulled out from under them. When things began to go wrong for Lord Mizuno, even he didn't escape a stab in the back; Torii stood to gain a higher political connection by it. And his hatchet man Inoue was not far behind him in cunning. As part of their plot to trap Takashima, they turned the spy Moheiji loose to follow him back to Nagasaki. All this came out later, when Torii and Inoue were themselves interrogated as criminals, but at the time they must have told Moheiji something like this: "Remember, this Takashima is only a city councillor, who wouldn't dare look the chief magistrate of Nagasaki in the eye, never mind government inspectors. He's always under pressure, see? So he's trying to get picked as one of the shōgun's personal attendants. That's how we can scotch him. Now if he happens to be interested in service with Lord Torii, let him know that our master would speak to Senior Councillor Mizuno about his career. If he wants a post with Lord Torii, he has to offer you some bait to work the deal for him, right? Then you bring it back to Edo and we expose him for bribery!

36

"On the other hand, if Takashima *doesn't* want to give the boss a gift, you can write a secret memo to the Bakufu saying you suspect him of plotting rebellion. As a commander of artillery and inspector general of public property, he's in charge of the forts at Nagasaki, so it's easy to hint that too many of his followers are in one place, they're manufacturing gunpowder, and so on. He'll have an arsenal, too. Everyone had a good look at his cannon and small arms on Tokumaru Plain. Why, it's only been a few years since Ōshio Heihachirō raised a revolt in Ōsaka, and all he had for firepower was old hand-me-down paper and glue jobs from before Sekigahara, back in 1600. Yet the roar of their muzzles was enough to make the country tremble. Wait till the Bakufu hears about Takashima's arsenal of modern Dutch weaponry, they'll know it's no joke! I can see it now—he'll be done for.

"Thirdly, try to sniff out evidence that Takashima is unsuited for his position. Find out everything about the fellow—we know he must be living in luxury, but get the details. Love affairs.

"Finally, we'll watch every movement of his ships and accuse him of secret dealing with foreign traders, Chinese or Dutch. . . ."

That was their scheme, and after Moheiji returned from Nagasaki, a secret accusation was made that would leave the authorities in no doubt that Takashima was disloyal.

His villa outside Nagasaki was backed by a hill of tall crags, and a stone wall had been built in front. You see, because his town house was destroyed by fire, he'd moved to this villa, the only home he had left. All his servants were now in the one location, and he needed various extra outbuildings and a granary. All this became, in Moheiji's secret letter, "a full-scale fort built on a good defensive site, with vast amounts of provisions, artillery, and rifles to distribute to his men, and a huge stock of gunpowder laid by for the day Commander Takashima has to withstand a siege. . . ."

At that time, Lord Izawa was chief magistrate of Nagasaki, and when he saw the report from Edo, he was stunned. How could he arrest Takashima on such trumped-up, not to say absurd, evidence? He looked into the matter carefully, and in his own report to Edo he gave the full story, saying it would be a rank injustice to accuse Takashima of treason.

When Lord Mizuno read this, he said the case didn't seem serious

37

enough to warrant an investigation, but Torii insisted it showed collusion between Takashima and Justice Izawa. Poor Lord Izawa! When Takashima went to jail, his superior was implicated, though he'd done nothing wrong, and relieved of his post; from magistrate of an important city he was demoted to caretaker of a castle moat and never regained his official standing. My Lord Izawa was an exceedingly fair and noble gentleman. He never blamed Takashima for his enforced retirement. After Takashima had been shut up for twelve years and received a pardon, the first to come and greet him was Lord Egawa, but the first person Takashima went to visit was Lord Izawa, to offer his apologies. Takashima said later that had his superior weakened in his stand and yielded to Torii's power, he might have been branded a traitor and burned at the stake.

Torii's defamation of Takashima was common knowledge well before his gang fell from power; but Takashima was not released even after Moheiji had disclosed Inoue Sadayū's machinations. Since he'd been accused of a crime on false evidence in the first place, to release him too easily would reflect on the authority of the shogunate. They didn't realize how that authority would fare among those of us who knew the whole story behind their arrogant manner and would never quietly submit to it. When Takashima was called for questioning, I went to give evidence, and you can be sure I gave them a piece of my mind. All I got for my pains was harsher punishment. The presiding official didn't even call me by name, but referred to me as "the traitor's depraved accomplice"! I was so scared at first, I threw myself down before the bench.

The judge began by saying, "You, the traitor's depraved accomplice, are charged with being disguised as a maid at the Nagasaki Inn in Hongoku. At that time, when you met officers on duty investigating Commander Takashima's stay there, you shouted out, 'Fire! Help, somebody. We're on fire!' and thus calling together a gang of street ruffians, did willfully and violently resist these officers. Do you deny this?"

"I do not deny it," I answered him.

It was true I'd treated their three spies like the scum they were.... I know I've told this story before, but after Takashima had left for Tokumaru Plain that time, these three rats came sneaking over to the Nagasaki to open his luggage and throw it around on the floor. Of course,

Inoue had put them up to it, in one of his foul plots. So I yelled "Fire!" and snatched the ledger they were reading out of their hands. They thumped me till my head swam, I can tell you. But when the firemen arrived, they got back double what they gave. It was only a little scuffle, but I had tied my fate to the unlucky Takashima, and now I was being mocked as his "depraved accomplice."

After the judge had passed a sentence of "severe reprimand," he began to abuse me, saying I was a rotten old harlot who had been deceived by Takashima. By now I was fuming, and I flung at them what I'd been thinking all day. When I lose my temper, you know, I really let go—not the way I usually am at all.

" 'Severe reprimand'?" I shrieked. "Thanks for the favor! Let me tell you something—I have never, not once, been deceived by Master Takashima. Oh no, it was a fox and a weasel who did *that*, wasn't it? Do you know who I mean? They crawled out of the same hole, wearing the same loincloth—with an Etchū pattern on it!"

"Shut up, you dirty slut!" the judge shouted at the top of his voice.

I had said too much. Etchū was almost Echizen and its "pattern" could only refer to its governor, Lord Mizuno; the "weasel and fox," of course, were sneers at Torii and his henchman, Inoue.

The judge was on his feet now, dancing with rage, and the constables beat me with their truncheons till I fainted. When I came to, I found myself shut up in a cell with a thickly latticed window, my arms and thighs red and swollen from the beating. When my welts had turned to bruises, I was dragged before the judge for another sentence. I'd got a "severe reprimand" before: now it was "life imprisonment"! My first feeling was resentment, not sorrow; but when I thought of Takashima never knowing how I'd come to grief, I felt so unbearably sad the tears came.

It was the fourteenth year of Tempō [1843] when I received my sentence of life imprisonment. But the year after, in the Fourth Month of the first year of Kōka, somebody set fire to the Kodemma prison. The part I was locked in wasn't burned, but it was customary during a fire to let everyone out for three days. Those returning within the parole period got time taken off their sentences. I took refuge at the Nagasaki Inn and rested the whole time. Genemon told me Takashima was likely to get exile or life imprisonment.

The innkeeper and his wife looked after me like a daughter, and made no fuss about my "crimes"; why, Mrs. Genemon herself massaged my weary bones from head to toe. Rather than call a professional masseuse and defy the law—the fox and the weasel again, in their Etchū loincloths—she did it with her own hands.

I said to her: "I'm so thin! The bones are sticking out all over me."

She tickled me playfully under the arms. "Don't talk nonsense. There's plenty of juice in you yet!"

Genemon watched us as he puffed on his pipe.

"You'll have to go back, you know, Oshima," he said in his kindly way. "If you go back willingly, the worst you'll get is exile, and with luck, no more than a reprimand. How would it be if I went with you when you go? Meanwhile, try to take it easy, just as if you were back home on a holiday. . . ."

The innkeeper was very worried about Takashima. Assuming he too had been let out because of the fire, Genemon expected him to seek refuge at the Nagasaki. But it seemed Takashima was determined not to trouble his old host, and we feared he might be spending his three days lying under a bridge. The innkeeper's business had gone downhill since his patron's scandal put the evil eye on it, and he no longer had the resources to send his neighborhood fire brigade on a search for Takashima all over the city. Other senior officials from Nagasaki visited Edo, such as Councillor Fukuda Kurōbei, who was at the height of his career in those days, but he'd never got along with Takashima, so he and his friends stayed away from the inn. In fact, the whole time I was there—three days and two nights—not a single other guest came to stay.

"I'm going into some other line!" Genemon announced. "Back to Nagasaki and open an Edo-style chophouse. The City of Flowers will be full of homeless beggars before long, their only shelter a rush mat draped over the head."

I remember those three days moment by moment, like the rarest of holidays . . . but the time finally came for Genemon to take me back to the prison. I stood in the hallway while his wife pressed a little package into my hand.

"Remember what they say: 'Money's a key that'll fit any lock,' including the one on the gates of Hell," she said and began to cry; I was crying, too, when a personable young samurai came up to the door.

"Do you need a room?" I asked, but all he said was, "I'd like to see the master of the inn. I'm Saitō Sankurō, a messenger from Lord Egawa."

My sixth sense told me he was bringing news of Takashima. But the deadline for my return was pressing, and Genemon had only time for a short talk as they were standing there. An urgent letter informing Takashima's friends of his firm resolve to return to prison had been delivered to Lord Egawa's mansion in the Shinzeniza district.

We thanked our samurai messenger and with many apologies prepared to leave, when without the least regard for rank, he came along with us, talking as he went. A broad-minded type not often seen in those days.

"My Lord Egawa said to me, 'If Master Takashima goes quietly back to prison, his punishment will be reduced considerably. I expect it will be commuted to medium banishment.' His very words!"

But as he walked along with us, our young friend had something more serious to tell us, something we hadn't expected at all. The man responsible for setting the fire was one Eizō, a fellow inmate of none other than Takano Chōei of the uptown school. Master Takano had taught him how to excuse himself from the crimes he was charged with, and in gratitude, it seems, he'd set fire to the prison.

The samurai bade us keep this to ourselves, and reassured us kindly: "Of course, there's no connection between Takano and Master Takashima. Absolutely none—I'm sure you people know that."

We parted on a street corner, and Genemon and I discussed what I should do after being sentenced to exile.

I didn't hear till much later, but after Takano was let out—like all of us, on parole—he eluded capture for three years! He fled first to Mizusawa, his hometown in the deep north, to see his mother, then on to Uwajima in Shikoku; after returning to Edo and drifting around for a while, he holed up in a house in the Aoyama district, where he was surrounded by the police, and finally cut his throat with his own sword. He had darkened his face with rock salt and changed his name to Sawa Sampaku. By that time, I had long since finished my term of banishment and was working as a geisha in Yoshiwara, where I often heard guests discussing Master Takano at parties. One story was that he'd killed himself. Another time, someone said he'd made his way to Okhotsk at the end of the string of islands off Ezo, and boarded a foreign whaler. Others said he'd hanged himself at the grave of Watanabe Kazan. There were even rumors he had come with a party of dissidents to Yoshiwara for an open talk and a good time; that's why so many spies turned up in the quarter around then. The feeling was that Police Chief Torii had become more active than ever. At times like that it gave me real pleasure to recite the old ballad of "The Seedling Seller" to my company.

It's sad that even a man as intelligent as Takano, once saddled with a crime, could be swept on to such a tragic death. He took his own life, I remember, on the first day of the Tenth Month in the third year of Kaei, and on the evening of the next day I heard the whole hair-raising story of his last moments from one of my patrons at a party. This was eight years after Watanabe Kazan, the leader of the uptown school, had committed suicide. And before them, Ozeki Sanei of the same school killed himself when he was accused of a crime against the national interest. What was it? Oh, he'd translated a book called *A Brief Account of the Life of Christ*. . . . Dr. Watanabe and Master Takano seemed to have told a few too many tales of foreign lands in their writings. Well, when I heard this story at my party that night, I asked the man who'd told it—a frequent guest, and a silk dealer from Takasaki by trade—whether this *Life of Christ* was so frightening a book?

My dear! He actually cringed, and in a nervous whisper said, "How would I know? I haven't read it—or even seen it. They'd crucify you for one look at it."

"You *are* a weak-kneed fellow, aren't you?" I said to him—but coyly, you understand.

"I love the way you said that," he joked. "Say it to me again when we're all alone. That'd make me even happier!" He was testing me, you see, as I was him.

"When will that be? After you've read the *Life of Christ*, maybe, and you're hanging on a cross?"

He passed his wine cup to me, and made me drink up five or six times in a row. I had a clear idea what was in his mind now, but he kept beating about the bush, and launched on a long description of how pretty the

42

roads around Takasaki were in early summer. He spoke of the hot-spring resorts at Kusatsu and Isobe, and wondered aloud if I wouldn't care to go on an excursion with him to Lord Ieyasu's shrine at Nikkō. I tried another tack, and after pretending for a while I couldn't make up my mind, I finally said I'd go with him to Okabe in the Bushū hills.

"You mean, where the post station is?" The silk dealer sounded hesitant. "Well, there's no hot-spring resort there, or any scenery, either. I always race through the place without stopping . . . but wait, they're supposed to have a fine temple in Harigaya, the Kōkōji."

"That's it!" I cried. "That temple—the Kōkōji. I'd love to go there."

After telling my lie, I stood up and went downstairs to drink some egg whites, then returned to the party. After egg white, you can drink as much as you like without getting tipsy—an old remedy, but it works like a charm.

After pretending to engage in a drinking contest, I made a pact with the silk dealer that was just the way I wanted it. The bargain was that when he returned to Takasaki, he'd take me as far as the Okabe station, where I'd wait for him until he picked me up again on his way to Edo. I knew it was a little selfish toward my sister geisha and all the younger girls, so I invented a cover story about traveling to a fashionable resort with my patron; my plan was to spend a little time in the hills of Bushū, relying on his travel money.

Of course, the truth was that it was at a camp in those hills that Master Takashima was being kept in "indefinite custody." I had waited many a weary day for a chance to see him, and now I was getting my wish. . . . At the time of the fire in the Kodemma prison, he'd returned within the three days and got his sentence commuted to house arrest on the estate of the Abe clan. When I asked Genemon at the Nagasaki, he told me the document with his sentence was terribly long-winded—hundreds of characters, he said—which meant the charges were not that serious! I didn't want to hear all the details, but the innkeeper put down the main points on paper for me.

> You, the accused, being favored with a prominent position among the officials of your native province, deserved exile to a distant island for your insolent behavior; however, since you honored your

parole after a fire broke out in the vicinity of the prison, your sentence is hereby commuted to "medium banishment." Nevertheless, since leaving you at large is deemed impractical, you shall be committed to the "indefinite custody" of Abe Toranosuke.

This Lord Abe was the local daimyō of the Okabe demesne. It was in his mansion in Edo that Takashima had first been confined, but, as you can imagine, there was too much gossip in the capital and it became a nuisance. So he was moved to Okabe. Besides, in Edo they felt the beady eyes of Torii and Inoue were always on them. From Lord Abe's point of view, it was no doubt easier to keep track of his charge in a place far removed from the capital. Then again, he might have wanted to keep more to the strict sense of "medium banishment," which required the culprit to be kept some leagues outside Edo.

I told my friends at the teahouse about my rendezvous at a hot spring, where I'd relax a little before setting off for Takasaki, and made myself out to the litter bearers as the silk-dealer's wife. This was early—before dawn, I remember—on the morning of the third day of the Fifth Month.

My escort may have been a sharp businessman, but as a ladies' man he was hopeless: just a rather common forty-year-old. Still, he told me he composed haiku and, when we reached Okabe that evening, pulled out his notebook and proudly showed me a few.

It was a depressing place, that post town; nowhere to eat but a little tōfu shop. The inn was of a sturdy enough plan, on a big scale, but not for guests, you understand—for silkworm culture. Our bedroom was right next door to a room full of silkworm trays with nothing but sliding doors in between.

I was very annoyed. "What a stink!" I said. "Is it the worms? How can I sleep?"

"It's not the worms." My silk dealer stayed under the quilts, flat on his stomach, but he lit a pipe and passed it to me. "Smells like mulberry leaves to me—like silk, in fact. What you're smelling is a hundred, maybe two hundred, bolts of new silk, all at once. It's not that bad, surely?"

All that day I'd watched a sea of waving wheatears float by on either side of the road; now I was sleeping with a man's loosened sidelock against my face, and its dry, musty smell caught in my throat like wheat dust.

We got up next morning and left the place together, saying goodbye at a signpost by the side of the road with the words "Kamakura Highway" carved on it. The plan was for me to make a seven-day pilgrimage to Kōkōji temple, where I would have a mass said for my poor mother, then wait for him back at the inn. We agreed to go back to Edo together. Of course, at that time, Mother was still in perfect health and living in Sen-ju: I added the bit about the mass for better effect. But after he gave me some money and said, "Here. Do justice to your mother's memory," I decided I'd better make that pilgrimage anyway, to atone for my sins!

Kōkōji was a huge place. A little off the Kamakura Highway was a dense, boundless forest of tall cedar and fir, and on the other side of it an ancient moat surrounding the great, sprawling compound of the temple. It didn't look like the usual sort: more like a retreat for scholars to study in peace. Peeping through the back gate, I could see no more than a dozen monks, young and middle-aged, gathered around the well. They were shaving each other's heads. A young novice, hardly more than a child, was stumping along the wall reciting a sutra in a low voice. He passed by the gate without noticing me, completely engrossed. It gave me a shock to see him, as though I'd stepped into another world; I turned away strangely depressed, yet deep inside I felt a rising exultation, as if my whole body were melting away.... When I asked at a farmhouse beside the main road, they soon told me where "Lord Abe's guest" was kept.

I spent my first fortnight in Okabe at a place called the Kawaguchi Inn. As you might expect, the post town itself was right on the main highway—the Nakasendō—but to the northwest of it lay the estate of a millionaire named Ruidai Gorosuke. It occupied the most prominent location in the area, sprawling all over the place like a giant snowman that had rolled there from a bygone age, getting fatter and fatter on every turn. I didn't know anything about it, but when I first arrived and was looking around for a proper place to stay, I noticed a pair of down-and-out samurai going in there, men I could see were free-wheeling spirits. Their shaven pates sprouted hair, their kimono hung in rags, and each had only one sword dangling from his sash, point dragging on the ground. They were rōnin, and no mistake! If the mansion was a port of call to tramps like that, I considered, chance could bring even Takashima along.

45

I decided to settle at the inn diagonally across from it, the one called the Kawaguchi.

But it turned out my guess was wrong. The story I had from the maid at the Kawaguchi, a woman called Okan, was that the father of Ruidai Gorosuke ("Generations," he was called) had been the broker for a kind of mutual credit association, and became a "mushroom millionaire" by running it like a loan shark and amassing huge profits; Gorosuke himself was a moneylender, too, serving the local samurai of the Abe clan. No wonder he had down-at-heels samurai calling at his premises. That kind of "credit association," run by vampires who bled their customers white with high interest rates and other trickery, had been ruled out-of-bounds by all the other clans a long time since. How I laughed at myself—to think of Master Takashima being the house guest in such a swindler's den! I asked Okan more about this Gorosuke, and got all sorts of details from her before I set out to visit him. I had a little scheme in mind, too.

The millionaire's estate was enormous, with five black-walled storehouses alongside the main house, and heaven knows how many behind; there was a great drum-shaped boulder by the entrance with a bronze sundial inlaid on top, and tied to an iron ring in its side with a red and white striped leash sat a rust-coated brute of a mastiff. On the earthen floor of the entrance hall, wide as it was, stood only a treadmill mortar. The lattice windows were of a *magaki* style you see in the Yoshiwara— with slats set far apart. The inner doorsill was at a higher level, and visitors could sit on one of the solidly built steps leading up to it. A man who'd come in before me—he might have been a farmer, about forty— was sitting there silently, with his head down. Another man who looked like the head clerk sat with his back against a screen. Neither said a word, but the farmer got slowly to his feet. He didn't bow and I thought he might be ill or something. Then he wound a dirty towel around his head and staggered out of the hall. I had brought a gold hairpin with me, and now I pulled it out and made my plea to the man by the screen:

"Excuse me, but are you the manager? I've brought this as security . . . perhaps I could get a small loan."

"I'm the one you want," he said, and took the pin with its wrapping from my hand. Then, "Wait a moment," he requested, putting on an Edo air, "I'll have to ask the boss—this coral looks like something special."

I'll say my hairpin was something special! The round ornament on it was the antique Chinese bead from the drawstring of Takashima's tobacco pouch. I told you how the jester got it off him by a trick—well, I'd bought it from the fool and taken it to a jeweler, who set it on a hairpin for me. It was as if I'd got it from Takashima himself, and that made it more important to me than anything else I owned. Of course, I had enough cash on me, and if I needed more I could easily have had my patron send a fresh supply from Takasaki. I was giving up my precious pin for one reason only: to strike up an acquaintance with "Generations" Gorosuke. I was traveling light, and a pin I could just pull out of my hair would look the most natural thing to pawn, without provoking suspicion. I thought it valuable enough to draw his interest. I was right. Out came Master Gorosuke, eager to do business, sure he could make a killing on my hairpin.

"A very fine piece you have here, miss," he said. "From Edo, aren't you? Where are you staying?"

"At the Kawaguchi Inn across the way," I told him. "Can you keep this pin for me? I'll come back to redeem it tomorrow evening, or the evening of the day after."

"No trouble."

I was afraid they might see through my act, so I deliberately asked for an outrageous price.

The clerk started shaking his head, but his master was quicker. "Work it out at the year-end rates," he said, and the clerk grudgingly opened the strongbox and made out a pawn ticket for me. Well! His "year-end rates" were enough to make your eyes fall out of your head. A week's interest added to my two days, *plus* service charge, if you can believe it.

"I'll be redeeming it tomorrow or the next day," I told him again, "in the evening."

"No. Sorry, miss," said his clerk—the weasel. "To us, you're bringing in the article on the thirtieth of the Twelfth Month, see, and that means year-end rates. Shop's closed up till the seventh of the First Month, and you have two days to go to New Year's Eve. That comes to nine days' interest."

He explained this as if it were the most natural way of dealing. For my money it was plain illegal, but what could I do? I'd taken the plunge,

47

and had to keep swimming! Thinking how to win Gorosuke over, I said in the voice I used to flatter my customers at parties:

"The sundial you have in your garden, sir . . . what an exquisite design! These Dutch-made marvels are all the rage even in Edo. How very chic."

Before returning to my inn, I even admired the leash he'd tied up his monster of a dog with: "Pretty as a picture," I said.

The evening of the following day, I was soaking in the tub when the maid came to tell me the head clerk from the millionaire's house was asking after me. Wondering what on earth he wanted, I jumped out of the hot water and went to see. Of course he'd come to dun me—what else?

"You said yesterday, miss, you'd be in tonight or tomorrow night to redeem your pawn. I came to remind you," he said. "You *will* be able to raise the money, I trust?"

"But surely I have eight days to go, counting from yesterday," I answered. "Didn't we agree on nine days' interest?"

"Adding seven days' interest at the end of the year is our standard practice. But the payment is due tomorrow night, as agreed—otherwise, I'm afraid, you lose your pawn. I'll come back tomorrow night, then. Good evening." And with an obsequious bow, he left me.

When I asked the maid Okan about this "practice," she said she too had borrowed money from Gorosuke, and paid the seven days' extra interest. The man wasn't just swindling—he was calmly robbing everyone blind. Yet the local authorities were prepared to overlook Gorosuke's activities as long as he didn't openly offend them. I depended on Okan's advice from the beginning, you see, because my plan was to use Gorosuke's connections to get a situation as cook in the military camp where Takashima was kept.

The first step was to get the head clerk on my side, so the next evening I asked Okan to make arrangements for a little saké party. But the creature was busy at some gathering of their vampire club, so his master came himself—expressly to get my money! I knew I'd never get another chance like this, and made Okan lay out the saké and treats right away. We warmed up a full half-gallon decanter, and instead of saké cups used tea mugs. For snacks we had chilled tōfu and bowls of crayfish boiled in soy-flavored stock, and for pickles, various sliced vegetables, radish, and boiled bamboo shoots dressed with raw soybean paste.

Gorosuke was in high good humor when he took his mug of saké from me, and said to Okan:

"What a splendid spread—I'm honored."

Okan poured oil into the lamp and lit it, saying "Please clap your hands if you need anything" before she left.

Tactful Okan! She was the same age as me and had once been a maid of all work in the Fukagawa quarter of Edo, as well as a nursemaid in a caterer's called the Rice Sheaf and a hairdresser in the entertainment section of Aoyama. She thought she'd seen me before somewhere, but the Rice Sheaf burned down just as I was starting my career, and wasn't rebuilt. The common bond of having lived in Fukagawa was enough for her; she was extremely kind all the time I was there.

Gorosuke made himself at home with the saké, but to my relief didn't try to act the fierce bill-collector and we hit it off splendidly. I spoke of the news I'd had of Takashima, of the favor he'd shown me in days gone by, and, of course, how much I wanted to see him again.

At that, he ducked his head down half in jest. "You don't know what you're asking! Favor is favor, and mustn't be forgotten—especially when it's of a gallant nature, but ... well, you should pay him a visit by all means."

My heart beat faster at his words, and I was flustered for a moment.

According to my guest, Takashima was confined in a cottage in one corner of the camp. Actually, it was more of a jailhouse. There was a small entrance hall, two rooms of only six mats each, a room with a wooden floor about four yards square, and a kitchen the same size; there were corridors on the north and south sides. A foot soldier called Kakizawa, a crony of Gorosuke's, was his warder. But the moneylender had never been inside the camp (he said) and had only heard of it from Kakizawa.

I'd been waiting for a lull in the conversation, and now I handed over the pawn ticket and the money. After I'd got back my hairpin, I disclosed my real intention. But when I said I wanted to be Takashima's cook, Gorosuke shook his head.

"That's a tall order. See, this camp is no ordinary camp, it's a fortress.

49

It's the military headquarters of the lord of Okabe—worth twenty-two thousand *koku* if he's worth one. A stronghold that covers twelve acres."

"If I disguised myself as a man, could I depend on your good offices?"

Gorosuke gave me a sulky look. "You want me to be your go-between, is that it?" He jumped to his feet and went out to the toilet.

When he came back, he suddenly sat down right next to me. I took hold of the decanter to pour him another drink, but instead he took hold of my shoulder. When I shrugged it off, he pushed me over and grabbed the toes of my *tabi* and jerked my feet in the air, forcing my legs apart. My god, it hurt! The pain was more than I could stand. I'd been in the geisha trade most of my life and I was used to these shenanigans, but never so brutal.

The decanter fell over, and without even thinking I clapped my hands and called out: "Okan! Okan-san! We've spilled the decanter. . . ."

Gorosuke dropped me as if he'd been stung and quickly sat down at the low table in front of the alcove. I sat up properly myself.

I heard Okan's voice saying, "Did you call?" and she slid the door open.

"Whoops! The bottle's passed out," she giggled. "Naughty bottle."

She mopped the spilled saké off the mat with her apron. Without drawing attention to it, she deftly palmed my hairpin, which had dropped in the fracas, passed it to me, and went out. Dear Okan.

"What do you mean, behaving like that? Were you going to string me up, like the rabbit did to the badger in the children's story?"

"What do you think I meant?" he said sourly. "There was no reason to call Okan. It'll be awkward for me if she wags her tongue."

Now don't knuckle under, Oshima, I said to myself, there's no need to send the man packing right away; and after I'd called in Okan to sit beside me, the three of us had a nice, relaxed little drinking party. The master of the inn was happy, too. He and his wife came in to pay their respects to Gorosuke.

"The wheat is turning out well this year, sir. Congratulations," they said, and bowed their way out. A strange kind of flattery.

Gorosuke got thoroughly plastered on the saké I plied him with. Like Takashima he was born in the tenth year of Kansei [1798], but looked years younger, about forty, with blue jowls and a blue shadow on his shaven pate. He was stocky in build, and his elegant silk *haori* coat with a Hakata sash and brown *tabi* suited him well. But it was only his sartorial appearance that was impressive: for the rest, his head and face were too wide, as if he'd been dropped as a baby. He looked like a catfish. Men with heads like that go crazy when they're drunk; I've been to enough geisha parties to know!

I was helping Okan tidy up when he dozed off. He was snoring like a trooper, until he woke with a start, and hurried home before Okan or the innkeeper could see him off with due respect. The innkeeper's missus was delighted, saying this was the first time they'd had the honor of seeing the millionaire drunk on the premises. Three days hadn't passed before the whole of Okabe knew about Gorosuke's binge at the Kawaguchi. Okan passed on to me all the gossip she'd heard outside. Honestly, you won't believe it, but I was being discussed as his possible concubine. The innkeeper and his wife treated me with great respect when they heard that.

Desolate as it was, the post town lay on a main road, and you could hear the latest from Edo fairly quickly. It was as good as a newspaper—better! You got details not only of which high officials were at daggers drawn, but what transpired in the highest councils of the shōgun. This was noised about the camp point by point, and the samurai knew very well their prisoner was now being treated with more lenience. We heard that Torii Yōzō had slandered Takashima's patron, Lord Egawa, to put him in a bad light with Senior Councillor Mizuno, but when his man Inoue tried to finish the job with more trickery, it blew up in their faces and left them without a shred of honor. These two were now such a stink in the nostrils of Edo that they and their spies and talebearers were quickly losing support from Bakufu officialdom. It was even hinted that Torii and company would be under house arrest soon—for life, some said. All this must have softened Takashima's keepers, until his confinement was slowly relaxed.

By this time I'd left the Kawaguchi Inn and was serving as a maid at an inn near the back gate of the camp called the Soldier's Rest. The mistress was a roly-poly woman of many talents; she cooked well, knew how to keep the customers happy, and had a tongue as smooth as honey. Her husband was a man of letters and a connoisseur: he could mount a scroll or a screen painting for you as easily as write a poem, and had won the patronage of Mochizuki Tasuke, warden of the camp. While I was still at the Kawaguchi, the old warden brought a group of out-of-town guests to the Soldier's Rest, and there, if I could believe the talk, my Takashima was surreptitiously brought to meet them. So I decided to move there. I asked Gorosuke for a reference, and he grudgingly put his seal on the arrangement; the master of the Kawaguchi took care of the rest.

Three months or so after I started work at the Soldier's Rest, Warden Mochizuki brought a traveler to stay with us. I happened to be absent just then, seeing my patron in Takasaki, but he was a retainer of Lord Egawa's, come all the way from Nirayama with a package from his master. Takashima happened to be indisposed, and his guard had to stand in for him and come to greet his visitor. The day I returned from Takasaki, I found that Lord Egawa's man had left that morning. The mistress told me that Takashima, on a field trip to Kushibiki Plain some while before, had tripped and sprained his ankle, and was still ailing.

Kushibiki Plain was a broad, desolate moor south of Okabe, wedged between the villages of Fujisawa and Hongō, and used as a firing range by the Abe clan. Takashima had gone there to inspect the firing drill and was giving some on-the-spot instruction in the placement of cannon when he hurt himself. The Abe people already had some old-model cannon in their arsenal, but they ordered some new ones from a blacksmith in Kawaguchi, who forged them to Takashima's specifications, to make up a dozen in all.

Rather than worrying about his accident, I was pleased by the good news that they'd relaxed his confinement enough to permit a visit to Kushibiki Plain. If that's the case, I thought, he'll be allowed out of the back gate sometime. That was where I could hope to meet him. In my elation, I got a little ahead of myself and started worrying about how I'd look for the occasion. I washed my face, hands, and feet carefully in hot water and did up my hair in a respectable, no-nonsense style. Still, I felt too excited to keep it to myself, so off I went to see my regular confidante, Okan, at the Kawaguchi Inn.

"Here I am again for a gossip," I said to her.

"I heard something that'll interest you," she told me. "Did you know your Takashima was getting massage treatment for his foot? Every day he leaves the service entrance of the camp and goes to a masseur called Sugaichi. I saw him yesterday as he passed by with his guard."

This masseur apparently treated clients at his house, on the edge of the forest. You got there by taking the back lane by Gorosuke's mansion. He would let you soak in bathwater full of mineral salts until you were thoroughly heated, then massage the affected joint and apply a sour-smelling lotion. Everyone in those parts swore by him. His patients came from as far away as Honjō and Fukaya.

I asked her, "Was he limping?"

"Only a little. He leans on the guard's shoulder and walks slowly."

"How does he look?"

"Pale. But not like a sick man. His eyes are wide open and he holds his head up. He has an honest face." She was kind enough to describe how he was dressed in some detail.

"Well, I'll come again tomorrow morning. I'd like a look at him from the second floor, if you'll let me."

From there I went straight to the masseur's place. The main building was thatched and looked much like a farmhouse, but the other structure, also thatched, was a partitioned longhouse. Attached to it was the bathhouse. It was summer, so it was open to the outside air, and I could see patients stretched out on the floor for a snooze, and others leaning against the wall. A matronly woman was lighting a fire under the bath. She looked up at the sound of my clogs and asked, "Have you come for treatment?"

When I said, "Could I have my shoulders massaged?" she led me to the main house and told me she was the masseur's wife. We found the master in dishabille, stretched out on a bench in the hall enjoying his siesta; when his missus roused him, he pulled on a kimono, tied the sleeves up with a cord, and strolled inside. He was a little man of fifty or so, with eyes sunk in his head like persimmon stones, so small they might have been stitched shut. But his starched kimono looked well on him, and he seemed to be a man of neat habits.

He took hold of my shoulders and began to rub downward.

"How does the lady prefer it? Shall I use the 'rough style'?"

When I said, "Gently, master, please," his fingers went to work very lightly and smoothly.

53

Quite casually I asked him how Master Takashima was doing. It seemed the trouble was in the upper tendon of his ankle. Playing into my hands, the masseur went on to speak of the conditions of his confinement in great detail. Originally slated for life imprisonment and treated like a criminal, he was gradually being accommodated with more consideration; although there were still bars on his windows, his position was now close to that of a house guest. His guard was really more like an orderly than a jailer. He had to follow Takashima whenever he went outside, but sometimes it was the guard who suggested they leave the camp! Again, when people concerned about the country's plight came from other provinces to see him, Takashima might argue with them, and there would be the guard, taking his side in the discussion like a loyal disciple defending his master.

The masseur heard this story from a young retainer of the Samura family, inside the camp. Master Samura's house was right next to Takashima's prison and had exactly the same floor plan. The young fellow had got himself kicked by a draft horse on the Nakasendō Highway, and had to be carried to the masseur's place for treatment.

I turned the conversation abruptly to another subject: "I suppose Master Takashima has lady friends somewhere in these parts?"

He went on kneading my shoulder. "I don't know anything about that, miss, but if there were several of them I'm sure I would have heard. Three or four women going in and out would be noticed."

"Is Master Takashima coming for treatment tomorrow?"

"No, from tomorrow I go to him. I've been given a pass to go in and out of the camp. It's in Warden Mochizuki's own handwriting."

How I envied that old man! While he worked on my hips, I turned over the possibilities, not sure what to do, but by the time he'd finished I'd made up my mind. When he went to give Takashima his treatment, he could take me with him.

I gave the masseur a big tip and said, "I have a favor to ask you. Master Takashima was my patron at one time. Could you tell the sentry at the gate you brought me along to guide you, instead of using a cane?"

To my surprise, the old man was willing to cooperate. "That's too much, miss. How can I accept a big tip like that?... Well, if you really want to go, I'd be glad to take you."

I trembled all over, I was so happy. After setting a time with him, I rushed back to the Soldier's Rest. I got a plan of the camp the innkeeper's wife had hidden away and pored over it, trying to fix the layout of the buildings in my mind. The fact that it was never meant to be seen by the likes of us made it all the easier to memorize. The main road ran straight from front gate to back, and on the east side of it, called "the barracks," were the offices and guardhouse. To the west lay the "upper premises": the lord of the clan's mansion, and the samurai quarters. These were surrounded by pine woods except where they faced the main road, and at the highest point in the northern part of the woods were the shrines of Inari, the rice god, and Suwa, guardian deity of soldiers. The whole compound was enclosed by a moat and a grass-covered dike. Looking from the north, from the Nakasendō Highway, you could see the white earthen walls atop them; on the other three sides, a palisade had been erected in strategic locations. Takashima's prison house was near one corner of the upper premises, just west of the mansion. I guessed that if you went in the back gate and along by the pine woods, you could reach it without getting lost.

The master of the Soldier's Rest always behaved as if he suspected a touch of hysteria in me. He gave me no orders directly, in fact spoke to me as little as possible; true, he didn't have much to say to his wife, either, but stayed holed up on the second floor of the storehouse mounting his pictures, or reading volumes of poetry; the scullery maid took him his meals there, and except for coming down to the privy, he hardly showed himself all day. He was a tall man, but lean and pale, like a green calabash. The mistress dropped vague hints as if she'd divined what I was up to—but they were nothing but shots in the dark, trying to get me to talk. I knew how easily my sweet secret could become known as "sex-madness" and kept it from everyone except Okan of the Kawaguchi. Even the masseur was given only the slightest hint of my real purpose.

No, I hadn't lost my senses. You see, all I wanted was to set eyes on him, nothing more. How can I describe the feeling?—the harder I try the more maddening it is to find the right words. It's like . . . well, you know when you want to look at your face in a mirror and there's no mirror around? That kind of frustration.

On the day we'd arranged, I jumped in and out of my morning bath

55

and pattered off to Sugaichi's house. I wore a plain kimono—with something a little more colorful underneath, of course. Still, I did my hair low, in a bun, more suitable for someone a blind old man would lean on. And for a hairpin—what else?—the gold one with the old Chinese coral bead!

The old masseur, his crown neatly shaven and wearing an unlined summer kimono, was sitting on the veranda puffing on his pipe. When he heard my wooden clogs, he knew me right away. "You're late, miss, you're late. Dolling yourself up, I'll wager—I can imagine how much time you take."

"Oh, no!" I said. "I just did my hair in a plain bun and came right over."

His wife saw us off, striking sparks with a flint—the ancient blessing to protect us on our way.

As we went by the Kawaguchi I called out to Okan, "Does this hairdo make me look too old-maidish—what do you think?"

She came out smiling and gave her kimono a little tug to show more nape above the collar. "I'd say it makes you look younger—and what a cheerful mood we're in today!"

Not a bad omen for my little adventure, I thought.

The Nakasendō went past the main gate of the camp, but I had to lead the old man along the edge of the moat and around to the back.

Crossing the bridge over the moat, we found a sentry standing, staff in hand, in the shade of a pine tree near the gate, which had an inner and outer portal. I showed him old Sugaichi's pass: "Blind Sugaichi, the masseur, and his assistant, to wait on Commander Takashima the gunnery expert, late of Nagasaki. Please let us in."

The sentry looked me over, mistrust in his eye. "The assistant has no business inside. I'll escort the masseur to Master Takashima."

"But officer," the old man said, "if you don't allow her in, I'll have trouble getting back here, as I can't see. Please let us both in."

"No! Can't be done." The sentry was brusque. "You can go in, sir, but your maid'll have to wait out here." He was an older man with a good-humored face, but his temper seemed to be getting worse by the minute. What could I do? I told the masseur I'd wait for him and went back over the bridge to sit on the grass beside the moat.

But the sentry yelled across, "Hey, you can't sit there. Stand up! You'll have to walk around if you want to wait."

So I had to walk along the bank of the moat to where it turned a corner, and back to the bridge, along the moat and back to the bridge, over and over again, the whole time I was there. I felt bitter enough, almost, to desert my blind friend and go home.

The camp brooded over me like a huge growth of forest; it hadn't been so before, but now I saw it as grim and forbidding, proof against all human feeling. It was partly the sentry's rebuff that made it seem like this. But it was natural, I suppose, that strangers couldn't just stroll in and out of a fort. The old man was given safe conduct not only because he was privileged to treat Takashima's ailment, but because he was blind and presented little danger.

The grass along the moat gave off a hot, steamy smell in the sun. The water in the channel had dried to a muddy trickle, laying bare the raw black soil of the banks; no stone had been used to reinforce them. I felt I was in a forlorn, unlucky place where no one passed, apart from the odd soldier slipping through the back gate. The other side of the path was nothing but fields, stretching away out of sight.

I got tired of waiting there, believe me. I'm the sort that flies off the handle if I'm kept waiting a minute. But perhaps it was precisely because waiting for my friend was pointless that I set my mind on it. A hot-tempered woman isn't happy unless she's got a good excuse to be impatient, you see! I suppose that's also why I waited so long for the day I could see my Takashima. Whatever you make of it, it wasn't the usual kind of love affair, was it?

I was musing on these things as I walked back and forth along the moat, when Sugaichi came out to the gate, and I knew I wasn't going to see Takashima again and that was that. By this time, I was so weary I was disgusted with myself.

When Sugaichi came through the outer gate, I saw he was led by a man of soldierly bearing, who walked him over the bridge.

When I went trotting up to greet him, he said, "I'm sorry I've kept you waiting all this time. But I have something for you," and he took out a little cake wrapped in paper from his sleeve.

"This is Master Takashima's warder," he went on, introducing the man beside him. "He was very nice to a useless old man."

The warder, Kakizawa, was a handsome fellow in his middle years; it was a shame, I thought, for such a fine-looking soldier to be a jail guard.

Acting on impulse, I pulled the gold hairpin from my bun and spoke to him. "It's too much to ask, I know, but . . . this hairpin. Would you give it to Master Takashima for me?"

"Hairpin? . . ." he said, then he understood. "Very well. But . . . shouldn't I give him your name?" He took the pin, which I had wrapped in paper. I didn't tell him my name.

"A long time ago, at Fukagawa in Edo, he gave his tobacco pouch with a netsuke of unicorn ivory to a certain man. Please tell him I bought the very same pouch from that man—and used the coral bead from its drawstring for my hairpin."

That was all. A little sentimental, you might think—but what else could I say? I didn't see Takashima again, after that. Ever.

John Manjirō:
A Castaway's Chronicle

Introduction

The Japanese have an apt word for their long insular experience: *shimaguni konjō*. It can be roughly translated as "insular nature" or "island mentality" and subsumes all that is strikingly different or unique in their culture. Whether their island culture developed the way it did from long isolation, or whether their original mentality was "insular" and sought a sheltered existence, is hard to say. But the fact remains that compared to other island cultures—most notably England's—the Japanese have tended throughout their history to seclude themselves and shut out external influence. Unlike the English, who have used their island as a base from which to launch bold forays into the outside world, the Japanese either ignored it altogether or let it come in on their terms. Absorbing foreign impact at their own pace, they allowed the outside world to touch their culture without disturbing its distinct identity. The oft maligned Japanese capacity for adaptation (or imitation, as it's usually called) and their gift for reducing foreign artifacts to fit the Japanese order of things is part of this survival technique. To most Japanese of the Tokugawa era, and perhaps even later, Japan was the whole world; everything beyond it was considered unimportant, barbaric, or downright dangerous. If this area of outer darkness had anything to offer the civilized people of their islands it could always be brought in, examined carefully, and absorbed into the Japanese life-style.

So the main direction of the culture throughout its civilized history was centripetal: communications and products from the outside world came flowing in and were either assimilated, remade, or rejected, depending on how useful they were for the Japanese. But toward the end of an especially strict period of seclusion, the 250-year-long Tokugawa era, it became increasingly difficult to keep the world locked out and the native population locked in.

It is true that the Tokugawa shōguns showed more wisdom and skill than Asian rulers elsewhere in keeping the early advance of European powers under control for most of their rule. But from the late sixteenth and early seventeenth century, when Spain and Portugal had unsuccessfully tried to Catholicize and subdue Japan, until the mid-nineteenth, the Western world had undergone drastic changes, while Japan remained similar to what it was at the end of the Middle Ages. Worse still, while the early shōguns (most notably Tokugawa Ieyasu) pursued a dynamic policy of playing one Western power against the other only to expel them all in the end, the nineteenth-century Tokugawas had no foreign policy to speak of, as the finale of "John Manjirō" clearly shows. Although the firepower of Spanish galleons was superior to that of contemporary Japanese vessels, an invasion of the islands would have been unthinkable in their time. The feudal rulers of Japan were able to send several hundred thousand well-trained samurai into the field, and to match such a formidable force was vastly beyond the logistical capacity of European navies. But in the 1850s, when this story takes place, their fossilized feudal system, with its political rule of thumb of "don't rock the boat," was facing a Western world where several major revolutions had occurred. It was utterly beyond the intellectual powers of the shogunate to analyze the far-reaching philosophical and political impact of the French Revolution and the tremendous advance of technology and military science during the ensuing Napoleonic wars. The dramatic emergence of new and powerful democratic nation-states—above all, the United States of America—remained an equally remote and neglected fact. But when one day in 1853 a great fleet of black vessels, each many times larger and heavier than the biggest Japanese house, sailed into the port of Uraga and aimed its huge guns at the harbor, the Japanese government could not ignore the existence of the West any longer. For better or worse, Commodore Perry's task force pried open the door of Japan and forced it to step into a modern century. By the same token, it was impossible to prevent a nation where ocean fishing was a major occupation from *any* contact with foreigners. Even if law-abiding Japanese boatmen observed the many prohibitions of their government, accidents still happened at sea. And so the earliest Japanese travelers to the West (albeit unwilling ones) were shipwrecked sailors and fishermen, such as the legendary Nakahama Manjirō.

The story of Nakahama or "John" Manjirō—as he came to be known during his American adventure—the poor, illiterate fisherman from Tosa who was to play such an important role on the political scene of these turbulent times, is true to history in its general outline: Denzō and his brother Jūsuke, young Goemon and Toraemon, as well as most of the Americans who appear in the story, are historical personalities, although Goemon was really Denzō's brother, not his son. Captain William H. Whitfield came from an old seafaring family and his forebears had sailed over to America with the Pilgrim Fathers on the *Mayflower*. In 1933, President Franklin Delano Roosevelt wrote a letter to Manjirō's son, Nakahama Tōichirō, in which he said:

> You may not know that I am the grandson of Mr. Warren Delano of Fairhaven, who was part owner of Captain Whitfield's ship which brought your father to Fairhaven. Your father lived, as I remember it, at the house of Mr. Tripp, which was directly across the street from my grandfather's house, and when I was a boy I well remember my grandfather telling me all about the little Japanese boy who went to school in Fairhaven and who went to church from time to time with the Delano family.... The name of Nakahama will always be remembered by my family, and I hope that if you or any of your family come to the United States you will come to see us.

So the historical background of the story is dramatic and exciting enough even without much intervention from the author. If Ibuse invents at all, it is in the small details of the story.

For example, when the castaways are stranded on a desert island where water is very scarce, their leader Denzō finds three buckets and establishes a unique system of storing water, calling them "wells." One, to be touched only in dire emergency, is called the "Well of Life," another becomes the "Well of Reserve" and the third, to be commonly used, the

"Well of Clear Spring Water." It is this finely crafted detail that gives the factual narrative its literary quality. Compared to the more experimental early works where Ibuse uses a variety of stylistic devices such as dialect, loanwords, neologisms and so on, the "classic" narration of "John Manjirō" is calm and simple, almost detached at times. And yet it is not just a dry retelling of a well-known Japanese legend. All the facts are there, to be sure, but so is Ibuse's unmistakable touch of humor. Take the hilarious scene during the castaways' trial, or official "debriefing" as we'd call it today. When Denzō and his men are ordered to stamp on Christ's image to prove that they have not converted to Christianity during their long stay abroad, the interrogating official inquires: "How did you feel when you stamped on the image?"

> "Rather cold," said Denzō, whose feet had become so accustomed to foreign footwear over the years that the bronze tablet chilled his bare soles.

The implied irony, the author's distrust of Japanese officialdom, and his sympathy for the common man and his pragmatic way of thinking are all trademarks of Ibuse's mature writing, and become even more pronounced in his postwar works. But what is most remarkable about this tale is the timing of its creation and its publication: imagine publishing a historical account of the close friendship between an American and a Japanese in 1937, a time when the wave of hysterical anti-foreign and especially anti-American feeling was reaching its highest point in Japan!

At a time when official communication between the two nations was breaking down, Ibuse recreated a true story about a dialogue that worked on a personal level. In an emergency, he seems to be saying, when the real issues of life and death are clearly stated, people of different color and culture who don't understand a word of the other's language will communicate surprisingly well. Using only gestures, the Japanese convey fairly complex facts and feelings to Captain Whitfield. The American skipper responds with equal skill and politeness. It is by deliberate design that Ibuse contrasts this smooth interracial exchange with Manjirō's failure to communicate at the simplest level with his fellow countrymen at sea:

After so many years, John Man was speaking Japanese again. No more in a dream, but in real life now, he called in his mother tongue as loudly as he pleased to fellow countrymen of his.

"What part of Japan do your boats come from? Are they from Tosa?"

"Sentei, Sentei," came the answer from the boats. Most probably it was the word Sendai, spoken in their local brogue. John Man had a boat launched at once, took two baskets of bread as a present, and rowed over to the fishing boats from "Sentei." Bringing his gunwale alongside one of their hulls, he passed the bread baskets to the fishermen. They accepted the present and opened the lids, but looked at the contents with suspicion. John Man spoke to a sturdy-looking youngster, who seemed to be the leader of the fishing party from "Sentei."

"Are your boats going back to Tosa?"

The sturdy young man looked puzzled, as if he couldn't understand his Tosa accent: "Don't know."

Ibuse uses polite standard Japanese to render John Man's words—not his native Tosa dialect—to suggest that with a willingness to communicate he could have been understood; but the Sendai fishermen are too frightened. Everything goes wrong during this encounter and finally Manjirō has to refuse a gift of bonito:

Then he [the young fisherman] picked up one of the bonito they'd caught and tried·to hand it over as a return present, saying "*Katsuo.*" Obviously afraid they might get into trouble, these men pretended not to understand a word of what John Man was saying. John Man gave up further attempts at verbal communication and simply gestured to them, "We've also caught plenty of *katsuo.* Thanks for your present, but I trust you won't get angry if I refuse it."

It is interesting to note that Ibuse does not use a Japanese verb when spelling out the content of Manjirō's gesticulated message, but says "*sono okurimono o* refuse *shitai kara. . . .*" To insert eloquent English words into one's native speech is a common habit of immigrants to an English-speaking country, but in this context it also subtly expresses Manjirō's rejection of the claustrophobic, exclusive Japanese identity. Although he does it politely, he is a free man now and can accept or refuse things—including some foolish rules of his native culture—as he pleases.

So the story has a twofold theme. It not only examines the possibility of human communication, but looks at the identity of the Japanese, posing the following questions: what happens when an "insular people" is exposed to a foreign culture? How viable is its identity in emergency situations? How well can it function outside the protective cocoon of its "island culture"? At a time when Japan was about to embark on its boldest confrontation with the outside world, these were timely questions.

Ibuse, a sober and lucid man, would be the first to reject a suggestion that his writing or his choice of these particular themes had any prophetic qualities. And yet good literature always points as much to the future as to the past. That he focused on incidents with Russians and on Russian behavior generally at the end of a story whose subject matter is the relationship between Americans and Japanese may be accidental, and it may not be. There were scores of such incidents with other foreign nationals, and the emphasis could have been quite different. There is another interesting symbolic parallel between the story and Japan's larger historical scene: John Man has lost his father, just as his nation will lose its "father"—the emperor, at least in his traditional "divine" role—a few years after the story's writing. And just as Manjirō finds his lifelong father figure in Captain Whitfield, as decent and modestly heroic a personification of his country's virtues as any American could wish, Japan, the shipwrecked boy on the turbulent waters of postwar politics, would face a historic choice: to join the Putyatins and the Muraviev-Amurskis or the Whitfields? True, there are also the Perrys and other American skippers, one of whom slaps Manjirō's face, treating him as a slave. The atomic bomb had yet to come, and Ibuse would later call it "the act of a vicious bully" in the words of Shigematsu, the protagonist of his major novel, *Black Rain*. And yet, all things considered, the story seems to suggest that it would most likely be Captain Whitfield's country with which the author would cast Japan's postwar lot.

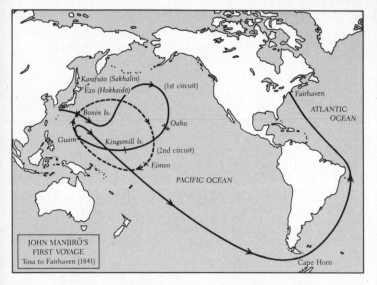

Karafuto (Sakhalin)
Ezo (Hokkaido)
(1st circuit)
Bonin Is.
Oahu
Guam
Kingsmill Is.
(2nd circuit)
Eimeo
Fairhaven
ATLANTIC OCEAN
PACIFIC OCEAN
Cape Horn

JOHN MANJIRŌ'S
FIRST VOYAGE
Tosa to Fairhaven (1841)

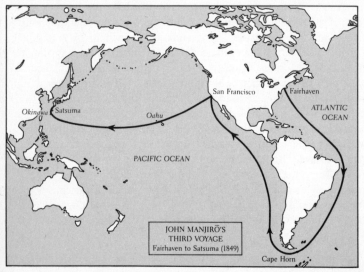

Okinawa Satsuma
San Francisco Fairhaven
Oahu
ATLANTIC OCEAN
PACIFIC OCEAN
Cape Horn

JOHN MANJIRŌ'S
THIRD VOYAGE
Fairhaven to Satsuma (1849)

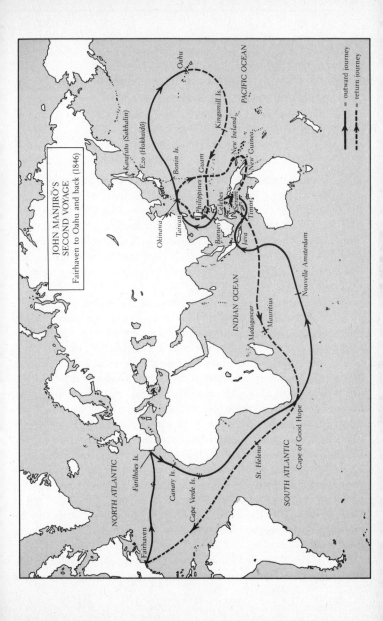

JOHN MANJIRŌ'S
SECOND VOYAGE
Fairhaven to Oahu and back (1846)

= outward journey

= return journey

PACIFIC OCEAN

Oahu

Kingsmill Is.

Bonin Is.

New Ireland

Guam

New Guinea

Philippines

Taiwan

New

Okinawa

Celebes

Seram

Borneo

Karafuto (Sakhalin)

Ezo (Hokkaidō)

Timor

Java

Nouvelle Amsterdam

INDIAN OCEAN

Mauritius

Madagascar

Cape of Good Hope

St. Helena

SOUTH ATLANTIC

NORTH ATLANTIC

Farilhões Is.

Canary Is.

Cape Verde Is.

Fairhaven

1

Manjirō and His Four Shipmates Meet with Disaster amid the Waves

John Manjirō's native place was a fishing village in the province of Tosa called Nakanohama; they say he was born in Bunsei 10 [1827], a Year of the Boar, but the exact date remains unknown. Manjirō's father, Etsusuke, died when the boy was only eight. His mother, whom they called Shio, had nothing but her own two hands to raise Manjirō and his four siblings when her husband died. They lived from hand to mouth, and one imagines she simply couldn't afford to have her children taught to read and write.

Manjirō had to go to work. Since the age of twelve or thirteen he rode on fishing vessels, struggling from day to day as a "fish remover." Hired on by various boats, he managed to earn a meager income. Just five days after New Year's, when he was fourteen, he set out for the first catch of the year, working as usual for one of the boat owners, Usaura Tokunojō. The crew consisted of four men besides Manjirō: Denzō (thirty-seven years of age), the son of Yōzō, a fisherman from Nishihama; his younger brother Jūsuke (twenty-four); Denzō's son Goemon (fourteen); and Toraemon (twenty-six), the son of another fisherman—Heiroku, from the same village. Denzō was the captain and helmsman, Jūsuke and Toraemon were charged with hauling up the fishing lines, Goemon worked the oars, and Manjirō unhooked the catch. With all the chores properly distributed, and about fifteen gallons of rice and the necessary supply of water and firewood in the hold, they sailed out of Usaura on the fifth day of the First Month, around ten o'clock in the morning. Their target was the sea bass known to gather in the early spring tides.

On that day they tried fishing out in the open, about twelve or thirteen leagues off Usaura, using a "stretching rope"; but since there were no fish around, when evening came they anchored their boat near Oki-tsu and, sheltered from the wind beneath Cape Yaso, awaited the break of day. They then cast their lines again in the open sea fourteen leagues off the Bay of Ashizuri, but as on the day before, they ended up without a catch. Like it or not, they had to abandon fishing and wait for another sunrise, dropping anchor near the shore.

On the seventh day of the First Month they sailed out again, some twelve leagues off Cape Ashizuri. But here too there was no sign of fish and a brisk sou'wester was gathering. As they turned back, about eight leagues from shore they encountered great shoals of mackerel and baby bream, surging from the water. Manjirō was the first to observe this throng of fish, so dense that the tide seemed to be dyed the color of their scales. Denzō the skipper urged his crew to pay out a full six buckets of stretching rope. They had hardly done so when the sky clouded over, and a sou'wester began to blow with sudden fury. The terrified crew tried to haul in the rope, not even waiting for the skipper's order. But the waves were swelling high as mountains and tossed the boat up and down like a float, so that retrieving the fishing gear was a far more difficult maneuver than they'd expected. After hauling in about three buckets of rope, they cut off the rest and decided to run for the mainland.

The wind was so strong they couldn't even turn against it, let alone hoist the square sail that had been provided for the boat. The rain came pouring down, and the men lost all sense of direction in the seething spray. Leaning on their oars with desperation, they kept rowing, but the boat flew before the wind like an arrow, driven by the battering gale. After much struggle, when the despairing skipper had managed to hoist a smaller sail, the mast broke. The crew lost their last ounce of strength, and collapsed in utter exhaustion. So the day ended, with their clothing soaked by the spray and the cold biting into their skin. When the rudder and most of their canvas were washed away by the waves, they were left with one oar. The crew had by now entrusted their fate to Heaven and lay sprawled on the deck, praying to their gods and Buddhas.

Morning came, and there was still no sign of the wind abating. It is a rule of the sea that if a storm doesn't lose its vigor by daybreak, it will rage throughout the rest of the day. By the time Manjirō ate his breakfast, urged by Captain Denzō, the boat was on the verge of capsizing. Fortunately there were no major breaks in the hull, and through the huge swell of the waves they caught glimpses of the land around Cape Muroto, however dimly, and even some houses. A watchtower called "Mountainview" was kept up on Cape Muroto, from which approaching whales could be detected at a fair distance. If only the lookout noticed them, he was bound to dispatch a rescue boat. The five fishermen began calling for help, spreading their arms wide and tearing their hair: "Help! Help! . . ." they shouted, but their craft was driven swiftly past, until they lost sight of the cape and of land itself behind the great shadow of the ocean. When their last oar was snatched by the waves, they couldn't even change course. Like a body with its arms and legs wrenched off, the boat was barely kept afloat with both masts lashed to the bottom of the hull.

Borne by the wind and currents, the boat drifted toward the southeast. A little past noon, they spotted the dim outline of some land on the port side. They thought it might be the mountains of Kii Province, but the next instant even this vision vanished in hazy clouds. They say a sailor has waves for his pillow, but Denzō's men felt they might come to rest on them forever. Toward evening a chill northerly picked up, and the men's clothes, soaked by seawater, began to freeze over, so that icicles were soon hanging from their sleeves and the knots of their belts. The five men tried to warm their bodies by burning planks from the ship's deck and the rush matting of their shelter, and finally endured the cold by huddling close together. Overnight, chilblains formed on the backs of Goemon's hands.

On the ninth, the wind was still blowing hard. The crew had eaten all their rice, but the fish they'd caught saved them from starving. The boat kept drifting in the same direction as the day before.

On the tenth, rain fell, mixed with sleet. It was even colder than the previous night, a day when the chill seeped into their very bones. Icicles hung from the men's belts and sleeves, and even Denzō's goatee had frozen solid. The sleet that landed in their topknots melted and trickled down their spines. By now the party had run out of drinking water, so they scooped up the sleet into their mouths and sucked the icicles. Goemon's arms and legs went completely numb from the hunger and cold, and he lay trembling under the matting, more dead than alive.

On the eleventh the wind and rain became stronger still. Denzō and

Toraemon spread a makeshift roof over the deck, using the remains of the sail. Then they chopped up some beams and planks, and nursed the ailing Goemon by the fire. They must have drifted far south of the mainland by now, for they experienced a little less cold on this day. They concluded that Goemon's illness was a feverish condition, caused by the acute cold, exhaustion, and starvation. The captain took a scrap of writing out of his amulet bag and put it in Goemon's mouth as a substitute for proper medicine. At length, the boy's fever seemed to be going down.

On the twelfth the rain abated somewhat. Around noon, as they searched the expanse of ocean, they spotted a vast flock of white birds. They knew these were what the fisherfolk of Tosa call *tōkurō* [or albatrosses]. Where these birds fly, they say, an island is bound to be nearby. The master, Denzō, pointed out the flying white host to the sickly Goemon, saying, "Look—*tōkurō*! Can you see them?" Goemon lifted himself a little, opened his eyes a mere slit, and traced the flight of the white birds. Then he lay face down again and burst out crying. Goemon was the same age as Manjirō, fourteen, but his spirit was a little weak for one born in the Year of the Boar.

The white birds slowly trailed off toward the southeast and vanished in the rain clouds. Denzō, Toraemon, and Manjirō surveyed the ocean's span, keeping a constant vigil. Toward evening, at long last they spotted the outline of an island lying straight ahead. Manjirō felt new strength flow into him. They raised one of the remaining beams as a mast, hoisted the square sail, and Denzō put together a rudder out of the ship's deck planks. With Toraemon and Jūsuke handling the sail and Manjirō bailing out the bilge, they steered for the island ahead.

When they reached the island, the sun had already set. Its coastline, as with so many desert islands of distant seas, was a sheer precipice which loomed like a folding screen. Huge waves broke at its foot, and the waters around were full of treacherous reefs. They couldn't find a single spot to drop anchor, let alone a proper harbor. To make sure, they sailed around the whole island, but all they saw was sharp, rugged cliffs rising steeply from the ocean. Nowhere could they find a stretch of sandy beach where they might land the boat. After midnight, the rain stopped and a hazy moon came out. In its dim light they could see a shoal of some reef fish swimming by. Suddenly their hunger and fatigue felt doubly

71

strong, and they got out their fishing gear in a hurry. They then sliced the freshly caught fish into sashimi and gorged themselves on the raw meat.

That night, they dropped anchor off the shore, at the limit of their anchor line, and waited for the dawn, eyes fastened on the island nearby.

The next morning, on the ninth day of their adventure, Goemon's illness took a turn for the better. Still, the weariness of the whole party was by no means improving. They seemed to have lost all their strength; just to lift the anchor, all five men had to team up. Yet as hard as they pulled they only managed to strain their backs and make their hunger worse. No matter how they tugged and heaved, the long anchor line stayed put, as if glued to the ocean's bed. The five men sat down for a conference.

"We don't even have a rudder now. If we stay on the boat, Heaven knows what tomorrow will bring. If we can land on this island, we might stand a chance of surviving. But it'll be courting death to try landing on those jagged cliffs."

After Denzō had pointed all this out, and his men had spent some time in deep thought, Toraemon said, "Either way, it's in fate's hands whether we die today or tomorrow. I'm in favor of throwing it all on one card and rowing toward the island."

Jūsuke was of the same opinion. Manjirō and Goemon agreed, too.

So Denzō joined together a few pieces of ship's timber and, shaping them into a device that more resembled a rudder, he decided that he and Jūsuke would try to handle it together. The other three—Toraemon, Manjirō, and Goemon—would use deck planks as oars, and beams from the matting shelter for poling; they then prepared to meet death together in case the worst should happen.

Denzō cut off the anchor rope with a hatchet. The boat began to move toward the cliffs, swaying wildly left and right. Avoiding the reefs, she approached a break in the cliffs, but then a massive wave swept her up and ran her against a jagged rock. In the same instant, Toraemon and Goemon, anticipating the impact, leaped onto one of its spurs; groping for footholds, they scrambled to the top. The other three tried to jump after them when a second breaker came crashing in. It rolled around the boat, turning her upside down and wedging her into the crevice between the cliffs. Manjirō was washed up on the crest of this wave and swept back into the ocean for a while; swimming madly he managed to catch on to the rock. Denzō and Jūsuke were thrust down into the crevice, both still clutching their makeshift rudder, and lay there writhing helplessly under the boat. Then a third wave came and lifted the craft in one effortless sweep, throwing both Denzō and Jūsuke on top of the rock, and leaving them there amidst the wave's froth and foam. "God, we made it!" they gasped happily as they crawled up the rock, searching for a better footing.

And so the five men's lives were saved. Only Jūsuke had hurt his foot hitting it against the pointed rock when the wave tossed him over. When the energy he had mustered to climb the cliff left him, he fell face down on the ground, unable to get up.

The boat they had left behind was smashed to pieces, shattered by the waves. It is a strange fact that a boat will never break up, even on the verge of destruction, as long as there is one last sailor clinging to her for life. It was because Denzō and Jūsuke were aware of this phenomenon that they had waited so long, rudder in hand, before abandoning their boat.

2

Manjirō and His Friends Yearn
for Rescue on a Desert Island

The island appeared to be about two miles in circumference and was uninhabited. Towering crags rose to the sky, one on top of another, and the only plant life they could find was a sparse growth of *kaya* grass. It made them wonder if the Mountain of Swords seen in pictures of Hell wasn't originally modeled on this scenery. But they had to find drinking water first, so the five stranded men parted company and set out in search of fresh water in the crevices of the rocks. What they found was a twelve-foot-square cave at the base of a rocky mountain overlooking the shore. Piles of seashells were scattered around its entrance and the men took this for a sign that humans had once lived there. Inside the cave, a rotten log lay with one end propped on a pillow-shaped stone as if it were sleeping. Just the place to make their temporary dwelling, the men decided, and lost no time cleaning it up. Then they went their separate ways again, and after searching far and wide one of them discovered a pool of rainwater in a rock's hollow. This little puddle would be their one and only precious well. Dipping their lips into the water, they quenched their thirst. But they couldn't find one edible thing—grass, root, or tree bark, except for a great flock of the birds called *tōkurō*, which came fluttering down along the cliffs. They managed to catch some with their bare hands and ate their fill of meat.

That night, they lay down to sleep inside the cave. But sleep wouldn't come, for a cold wind blew in through the entrance and they had no mats to protect their bodies from the chill. Guided by moonlight, they went down to the shore and gathered what they could of the flotsam that had drifted there from their wrecked boat: canvas, boards, and the like. Taking it back to the cave, they put up a door of sorts to bar the entrance. They then took off all their clothes and made a single rough mattress on which they huddled together, bare skin to bare skin in one tight knot. But they still felt restless, if not from cold then from an unbearable sense of loneliness. They felt they had to speak to each other:

"What's the name of this island, do you think?" said Denzō. "It's pretty far south, but too cold to be a southern island. Maybe it's cold because we drifted too far east."

If a man as steeped in the ways of the sea as Denzō was at a loss, how could the others know?

"Are we still on Japanese territory?" asked Toraemon. "If it's east enough to get as cold as this, it must be even farther east than Izu. But I've never heard that the farther east you go the colder it gets. Isn't the End of the World in the north?"

"The End of the World," explained Denzō, "can be found in all four directions, if you go far enough north, south, east, or west. No, I don't think this island is near the End of the World, but we're dreaming if we expect a rescue boat in these waters. We've landed here now, and this is where our bones will rest. Then again, why not look at our day of arrival here as the First Day of Creation? Why don't we all cheer up and look at it that way?"

Why not indeed, thought the other four, and heartily agreed with Denzō's proposal. And so, to put it in contemporary terms, the day of landing became the first day of the first year of the Desert Island Era, and the men all vowed to value their lives and abandon any unnecessary doubts about human existence.

Thus the following day, the fourteenth of the First Month, was the second day of the Desert Island Era. As soon as the five men woke up, they left the cave to forage for food. The weather continued stormy and it was too dangerous to gather shellfish on the shore; they went to catch albatross again, although the taste of its meat was much inferior to that of the shellfish. The birds swarmed around the island in such multitudes that its rocky peaks looked snow-white and they made no attempt to flee when human beings approached them. Catch one, wring its neck, catch another, wring its neck . . . so went the routine, and in less than an hour the men had killed more birds than they could carry back to the cave. When they got there, they sliced up the meat with the nails they'd salvaged from washed-up planks, and what was left of their meal was

75

pounded with stones and dried in the sun. They called this dried meat "stone-fried" and, to change its taste a little, preserved it in salt.

Denzō brought home three small buckets that the waves had washed up near the shore. He made lids for them out of *kaya* grass and called them "wells"; they'd serve for storing their rainwater. The one that looked newest, a pail used for washing rice, got the name "Well of Life." The one shaped like a measuring box, with the character *Yamajū* branded on it, was called the "Well of Reserve," and the third, which was shaped like a saké barrel, became the "Well of Clear Spring Water." Denzō then laid down a solemn law concerning the use of water from these wells: even if it rained and the buckets were brimming full, one mustn't drink "well water" as long as there was some rainwater dripping into the hollow from the rocks. When sunny weather continued for some days, the water in the hollow would soon dry up.

That was the worst thing: they couldn't drink their fill of water. In the first month after landing on the island, they didn't have any rainfall for ten or even twenty days in a row. Needless to say, the water in the hollow soon evaporated and they ended up drinking not only from the "Well of Clear Spring Water," but from the "Well of Reserve" and finally the "Well of Life," too. To moisten their mouths, the five men chewed on grass stalks, sucking out their juice, or licked the rocks wet with the night's dew. After this bitter experience, Denzō added the following strict rules to his "water law":

Article I. Never waste water. Stealing water from the wells and drinking it on the sly is strictly forbidden.

Article II. After a meal of albatross, each man will be allowed one oyster-shell of water. He should strictly abstain from drinking any more.

Article III. Water is not to be used with a meal of seaweed. The weed must be thoroughly cleaned of salt, and saliva is to be swallowed copiously while eating.

So went the rules, but as none of Denzō's men could read or write, he had to instruct them orally until they had the rules by heart and came to observe them with proper reverence.

They had all become terribly emaciated, reduced to mere shadows. Their food consisted solely of albatross meat, seaweed, and shellfish, and they had to eat it all raw. Their flint and tinder, pots, kettles, and other cooking utensils had been washed away by the waves when the ship went under. Trying to start a fire, Denzō threshed some withered *kaya* grass until he had a fine, cotton-like substance. Then he struck it time and again between two stones against a nail but, however hard he tried, it was useless.

The albatrosses which once hadn't fled at their approach were getting wary. They would let the men come within five or six feet, then hop away. If pursued, they'd take to the air and be gone. So the men had to lie in ambush behind the rocks and take the birds by surprise, clubbing or stoning them to death. But the *tōkurō* soon learned to watch out for people and withdrew way up into the steepest crags. They also began laying their eggs in deep crevices where human hands could never reach. And finally, by the end of the Fifth Month, when their chicks had left the nests they flew away from the island at the head of their young ones.

It was at this time that Denzō had a serious accident. Climbing up the rocky peak that loomed in front of their cave, he spent the whole day hunting for albatrosses; all he got was two birds. Throwing his booty from the cliff toward the entrance of the cave, he started back down the rocky slope, but his foot slipped when he was still more than ten yards above level ground. Fortunately, he managed to get a hold on a clump of *kaya* grass that grew about halfway down the cliff, and though his body was badly bruised all over, he was able to make it down the slope and back to the cave. But as if the mishap had broken his spirit, he grew despondent, lost even more weight, and sat all day long brooding inside the cave.

Denzō's brother Jūsuke, whose leg wound wasn't healing, also spent most of his time in the cave, nursed by his elder brother. Goemon and Toraemon, though not actually sick, looked even more wasted than the real invalids and spent their days in deep gloom.

And so Manjirō alone was in fair shape, body and spirit alike. On occasion, he took grave risks—such as the time when he went to investigate

77

the highest summit on the island which no one had dared before. The craggy peak wasn't much higher than a thousand feet, but the other men had given up hope of climbing it, concluding, "You'd have to be a monkey to scale a peak like that." But Manjirō climbed it, clinging as close to the rock face as he could. There was a wide stretch of level ground at the top, where he found a stone-covered well and two slabs of rock which looked like tombstones. A little pool of muddy water remained in the well and the tombstones were badly weathered. Manjirō lingered there for a while, then happened to look out to sea. There—swimming playfully in the tidal currents—he saw more than ten whales.

When he returned to the cave, he reported his news about the well and the tombs to Denzō and the others. Denzō asked him if the tombstones were overgrown with moss and then, probably feeling homesick, covered his face with his hands. Both Toraemon and Goemon started crying too. After a while, Denzō stopped crying, but when Manjirō told him about the school of whales he'd sighted, he burst into tears again: "Manjirō, it's a crime to talk about such things. . . ." No doubt the thought of stuffing himself with whale meat was too much for Denzō.

But then on the seventh or eight day of the Sixth Month, something unexpected happened that brought them great joy and ended the long spell of bad luck. Early that morning, Manjirō had gone down to the shore and, as he was gathering shellfish, far off in the east he noticed a black dot, about the size of a bean, on the ocean. It had to be a ship! Manjirō danced a jig and started shouting at the top of his voice:

"Hey, Goemon, Toraemon—a ship, a ship is coming!"

Goemon and Toraemon had arrived at the shore a while before to look for shellfish; now they ran toward Manjirō at top speed and, glancing off to sea, danced their own jig of joy. It was a ship for sure! And her course seemed to be set straight for the island! It was a foreign sailing ship, her three masts full-rigged with an array of sails. She came so close they could observe people in pipe-sleeved jackets walking the deck. But all of a sudden, she changed course toward the northwest for God knows what reason and made to pass them with utter indifference. The three startled men rushed to a little hill nearby, yelling at the top of their lungs that there were castaways on this island and begging the ship to return. They picked up a length of ship's timber that had washed ashore and, tying Toraemon's checked undershirt to one end, waved it high in the air.

The foreign ship seemed to get their meaning, for she came about and headed for the island. About two miles away, she dropped anchor and dispatched two longboats with a crew of six in each. As they rowed toward the island, the castaways waved their hands to beckon "Come on, faster, faster," and some men in the boats took off their caps in response and waved them all the way to the shore, as if inviting the stranded men into their boats. But as there wasn't a stretch of open beach where the longboats could land, the foreigners in the boats showed them by gestures that they should take off their clothes, tie them in a bundle on top of their heads, and swim over. The three men on the cliff hesitated, a little frightened by the strange sight of people unlike any they'd seen before, with red hair and blue eyes. Then Manjirō summoned up his courage, stepped down from the cliff, and did as the foreigners had instructed: taking his clothes off, he tied them to his head and jumped into the ocean. The foreigners rowed their boat nearer and, taking Manjirō by the hand, helped him climb aboard. Manjirō felt as if God himself had come to his help and his heart overflowed with gratitude. But when he fell on his knees and began worshiping the crew, the black-skinned sailors among them burst into booming laughter. Soon Goemon tied his bundle of clothes to his head and swam over to Manjirō's boat; he too was helped aboard. The last one to join them was Toraemon.

In their excitement, the three men had completely forgotten about old Denzō and Jūsuke, who were left behind in the cave and knew nothing about the ship. Toraemon tried to explain the situation, but since his words weren't understood, he pointed to the cave and gesticulated that two men were still left there. At that point the negroes were given some kind of order and started rowing one of the longboats back to shore. Denzō had just been wrapping a cloth bandage around his brother's sore foot, when all of a sudden a pitch-black human stepped into the cave, uttered the weirdest-sounding gobbledygook, and tried to drag him out. Denzō was so startled he brushed the man's hands away and made to dash out of the cave, but then a white-skinned foreigner came up and tried to convey something to him with gestures. Denzō interpreted them to mean:

"Take it easy, take it easy. We're not going to hurt you. Your friends have already been saved by our ship. There's nothing to worry about. We're all brothers of the Four Seas."

The white-skinned foreigner smiled in a good-natured way. The dark-colored stranger also smiled, displaying an awesome row of white teeth. Denzō felt greatly relieved. Exchanging glances with Jūsuke, he followed the men down to the shore. Jūsuke was the last to leave, not walking but carried in a pair of strong black arms. And there they were: in one of the longboats, gently swaying on the waves, they saw their three friends, sitting upright and looking slightly bashful.

Denzō obeyed the gestures of the white foreigner and, taking his clothes off and tying them to his head, jumped into the ocean. The black foreigner caught Jūsuke in a bear hug, a rope was tossed over from the boat, and they were both safely towed aboard.

The white foreigner then asked them in sign language:

"Have you left any valuables in the cave? Don't hesitate to tell us. We'll send these black men to get them."

Denzō gesticulated back: "What valuables would castaways like us have? The most precious, most moving thing that ever happened to us here was being rescued by you...."

"Well, the pleasure is ours as much as yours. But surely you left something behind. Feel free to tell us."

"Some clothing, feathers, a turtle's shell, dried albatross meat, and other odds and ends of that kind, that's all we left back there."

The white foreigner gave a resolute nod and issued orders to the darker ones. Synchronizing the rhythm of their oars, they swiftly rowed the longboats toward the ship waiting in the offing. They went at least three times faster than a similar five-oared boat of Japanese make.

They reached their ship toward evening, when the setting sun was just a few minutes above the horizon.

3

Manjirō and His Friends Sail Farther
and Farther Away from Home

The ship that had rescued Manjirō and his party was a steel-clad colossus, 180 feet long and thirty-six wide. Her three masts were rigged with at least a dozen jibs and sails and spread a spider's web of ropes and rigging all around the ship. Above the bulwarks, whaleboats hung from their davits at regular intervals; three along the port and another three along the starboard side. On her stern, the ship flew a flag dotted with bright stars. About thirty men, both black and white, made up her crew. This huge vessel was a whaler called the *John Howland*, and her home port was New Bedford in America's state of Massachusetts. The skipper, whose name was Whitfield, summoned Manjirō and his friends for an interview. The entire crew stood at attention in a solemn straight line, and when Manjirō and the others saw this imposing formation they were so overwhelmed that they fell to their knees in front of the captain. But the captain said something in his foreign gibberish, motioning freely with his hands. It seemed to Manjirō that he was trying to tell them:

"Oh no, you don't have to kneel before me. I'm not a priest with a cross around my neck ... please get up, do get up!"

When Manjirō and his mates rose to their feet, the captain took a little notebook and a pencil out of his pipe-sleeved jacket. He made a rough sketch of a boat, then added a mast and pointed to Manjirō's face, then again at the picture. Manjirō thought he might be asking:

"The boat you see here has one mast. What I'm trying to find out is, did your ship also have one mast?"

Manjirō nodded. "Yes sir, you're absolutely right."

"Ah, Japanese, Japanese," the captain exclaimed delightedly.

More gesturing and questions in the outlandish lingo followed; the captain seemed to be asking, "How many years did you spend on the desert island over there? One year?—two?—three?—four?" He counted on his fingers. "How long could you have lived there?"

Denzō drew the shapes of a new moon and a full moon with his fingers, and then showed the number "six" in the way children often do with their fingers.

The captain nodded with a smile, and pointed to the bow, as if to say: "You need a good rest, men."

He then gave a brisk order dismissing the trim line of sailors standing behind him.

This captain and his crew seemed to be kind people. Manjirō and his companions retired behind a large coil of rope in the ship's bow and set about changing the bandage on Jūsuke's foot. The pain seemed to come from a muscular spasm caused by the bruise—the muscle's ligaments were probably torn from the bone. Jūsuke complained about the pain, saying: "When we were standing in front of the captain, I felt I couldn't bear it any more, but I knew I had to—that man had the dignity of a chief magistrate in Japan."

They were just telling each other how famished they all were, when one of the black foreigners brought a wooden bowl heaped with baked potatoes and gestured, "Eat this." The potatoes tasted like manna, but they had barely managed to swallow a few when all of a sudden a white foreigner came running over and snatched the bowl away. He took the black man aside and gave him what looked like a severe dressing-down; then he went away, looking very upset. What a cruel thing to do, thought the party of Japanese, resenting the white sailor. But in a while the same man whom they'd thought so hateful brought them some meat stewed in flour gravy and gestured, "Eat this." Now this is really manna from Heaven, thought the castaways, and fell upon the meat. And then the man came for a third time, bringing a bowl of steamed white rice and urged them, "Eat this, too." But neither the gravy nor the meat and rice were served in sufficient quantity, and the men couldn't eat their fill. They didn't realize that the foreigners were taking a kind precaution, for when starved men take in a rich meal too suddenly, they can drop dead on the spot.

The next morning, on the eighth or ninth day of the Sixth Month, the captain ordered the black men to launch a boat and bring some of the clothing, bird's feathers, and the giant turtle's shell from the cave back to the ship. The castaways thanked the captain from the bottom of their hearts for his kindness, although their moldy old clothes and smelly feathers seemed of little use to them now that he had issued them with pipe-sleeved jackets and leather boots. The neatly fitting jackets didn't feel bad at all, but their new leather boots were quite uncomfortable.

A little before noon that day, the ship weighed anchor and set sail for the southeast. The five men were shown into an eight-mat cabin below and told they'd better take it easy for a while. Three days later, they had recovered their spirits, and in five days their bodies were back in shape. They'd really be taking advantage of providence, they thought, if five able-bodied men like them kept loafing around, and so on the seventh day they told the captain they were ready to help out with the crew's work. Jūsuke's wounded foot was getting better too, thanks to the care of the ship's doctor. He had diagnosed the ailment as something called "our-foot-sore" or "your-foot-sore."

The doctor applied an acid-smelling ointment to the sore part, covered it with oilpaper, and then wrapped a strip of white cloth around it. The ailment was getting better by the day and Denzō and Toraemon's admiration for the doctor's treatment of it knew no bounds. Yet they were still a little puzzled by the disease—something called "our-foot-sore" or "your-foot-sore" couldn't have come from an ordinary bruise.

On the eighth day, the ship changed course toward the northeast and on the ninth turned southeast again; finally on the tenth day the lookout in the crow's nest spotted some whales with his telescope and gave the long-awaited signal. Manjirō hurried to the deck. Far off to the south he saw a school of whales, raising white waves as they cut through the water. The ship followed the white wake and, when she was about fifty swells away, came about and shortened sail. The six longboats were lowered swiftly into the water, the six-man crews climbed down the rope ladder hooked to the gunwale, and they all rowed out in pursuit of one whale they'd singled out. No one was left on the ship except the doctor, the cook, and Manjirō's party.

The six boats flew ahead, each competing for the lead. One was a little faster and overtook the others by about two swells. In its bow stood the harpooner, his weapon at the ready, waiting for the next wave to lift the boat high; when it came, he hurled the harpoon at the whale with a whip-like crack of the line. Then the boat cut sideways through the rolling waves and headed back for the ship, paying out lengths of loose rope to the harpoon. The whale took off with it and began towing the boat over the waves in a wide circle of about three hundred yards. Harpoons came flying in succession from the other five boats. The whale thrashed about like mad, raising huge waves. Then its body emerged halfway from the water like a weird rock towering from the ocean's depths. One of the harpoons had pierced its heart. The whale spouted a pillar of blood from its blowhole, and soon lost its fierce vitality. As if abandoning itself to the waves, the huge body rose and fell with their swell, until it slowly rolled over on one side. Several sailors jumped onto its back, dealt it a finishing blow, and tied a thick cord around its tail fin.

Manjirō and his friends watched this whaling spectacle from the ship's deck, barely daring to breathe. They were all deeply impressed and it was clear to them that their sea-bass fishing back home was mere child's play compared to this. They say in Tosa that when you catch one whale, seven seaports will flourish; if only they could use the foreigner's way of taking them, not seven but seventy ports might thrive.

The longboats towed the whale back to the ship and its carcass·was tied to one of the bulwarks. Manjirō's party, trying to stay out of the busy men's way, watched the ensuing operation from one corner of the deck. The whale's body was lifted by pulleys and cut up into round slices. The skin was stripped off with long, halberd-like knives. Each of these procedures followed a regular, well-timed pattern. There was even a man in charge of spreading fresh sawdust on the deck, and another who mopped it up once it became soaked with blood. There was a team that specialized in carving up the whale's skin, one that boiled down the fat in a large cauldron, another that poured it into barrels, and still another that hauled these down into the hold. With all the various chores carefully distributed, the whole operation was performed with the utmost dispatch, down to the final dumping of the whale's meat into the ocean.

Her job completed, the ship set sail again for the southeast. A large flock of seagulls followed them till nightfall, attracted by the smell of whale meat that permeated the whole ship.

The next day, it was Manjirō who kept watch on the masthead. As he peered through his telescope, he spotted two whales, a mother and its baby, floating on the waves. The older whale tried to get away, shielding the small one with its breast fin, but the harpooners in the longboats chased and killed it the same way as the day before. They let the baby whale get away unharmed.

As a reward for sighting the whales, the captain personally presented a brand-new sailor's cap to Manjirō. Denzō, Jūsuke, Toraemon, and Goemon, who had carried barrels of whale oil into the hold and mopped up the bloodstained deck, were given similar caps for their efforts.

The ship kept a steady south-southeast course and by late December, after six seaborne months, she reached a harbor called Honolulu on Oahu Island in the Sandwich archipelago. On her half-year cruise the ship had harvested fifteen large whales.

For the first time in a long year Manjirō and his companions were feasting their eyes on a stretch of land that looked like *terra firma*, and were longing to set foot ashore. But the captain summoned them and explained in sign language:

"Now listen to me, men. I'm going ashore to visit the governor's office and take the necessary steps for you to be allowed to land here shortly. Wait for a while before you disembark, and I'll try to get you a place to stay."

Denzō gestured back, as the spokesman of their party, "This is all fine with us, Captain, and we're deeply grateful."

"I'm afraid that even after you get your landing permit, you'll find it hard to make a living at first. You should be given some kind of allowance from the governor's office, at least for the time being."

This skipper was a kindhearted man, and a very straightforward one. Even when he had to take one of his deckhands to task, he'd look the man straight in the eye, snap out a word or two in his outlandish tongue, and in a moment his face would be as calm and composed as ever. The men were all devoted to him and went about their chores quite cheerfully.

Manjirō and his mates were left on the ship, awaiting the captain's summons. Every so often they'd put their heads together and discuss plans for the future, especially what to do with their lives once they were allowed to land. One thing was certain: they'd have to learn the foreigners' language, and so they asked the sailors minding the ship to teach them how to pronounce some common words. Perhaps it was his age, but Denzō was the slowest to learn, Manjirō the quickest by far.

The crew took their shore leave by turns and many returned to the ship in their cups. The captain, it seemed, had a good deal of business on land and it was over a month before he summoned Manjirō and his friends. Led by Mr. Whitfield, they all went ashore and called on the governor in his office.

The governor was a fifty-year-old American by the name of Dr. George. He had practiced medicine back in America, they were told, then came to the islands to try his luck; having gained popular favor, he was later elected governor. Dr. George brought out a map of the world—something neither Manjirō nor his mates had ever seen before—and unfolded it in front of them. Then he pointed to various places on the map with his finger and asked the Japanese party in simple language:

"Is it this place or that one? Were you born here or over there? Or perhaps here?"

Manjirō, who already understood a little of their language, replied on behalf of the others, "We don't know. What is this large sheet of paper?"

The governor couldn't conceal a smile and explained politely, "It's a folding map. Look here, all of you: this is the ocean. This is a large continent. This is an island. Is the country you come from around here, or could it be over there?"

"We are Japanese," Manjirō replied.

The governor exchanged glances with the captain who was sitting nearby, and they both nodded. Then he joined his hands as in prayer and made the gesture of worshiping a deity.

"Do you worship gods and Buddhas?"

"Yes sir, we do," they all replied.

The governor walked over to a cupboard, took out a Japanese pipe, one gold piece, twenty pieces of silver, and a copper coin from the Kanei era. "Do you know what these are?" he asked Manjirō.

"These coins were made in our country," Manjirō said.

"All right, then let me ask you: do you know a place called Ōsaka?"

"I do."

"What kind of place is Ōsaka?"

"I haven't been there myself, but Denzō here knows it well. They say Ōsaka is a well-known port and a very prosperous place."

"So it seems. I understand it's the best port in all of Japan. Well, now that we know you're Japanese, I'll tell you about these things. This long pipe and the coins were given to me fourteen years ago, when a merchant ship from Ōsaka drifted to Oahu's shores. The crew were all charming fellows. Upright and sincere, just like you. I expect we can support you from public funds for a while. In the meantime, you'll need some pocket money. Here, let me give each of you a personal gift of one silver dollar."

Manjirō lowered his head in gratitude, bowing as humbly as he could. When they had all received their silver piece, they were shown into a waiting room and served some long, cone-shaped fruit and drinks of a brownish color. The five Japanese were then provided with everything they needed by the governor's office: lodging, clothes, even food. Perhaps the Hawaiian government's policy was especially generous at the time, but Captain Whitfield's forceful recommendation certainly went a long way. The captain not only took pity on the Japanese castaways, he came to like their honesty, diligence, and sharpness of mind, which they all had in common. Most of all he was fond of Manjirō for his cheerfulness and courage, and seemed quite sorry to leave the boy behind in Honolulu. At last he asked a certain S. C. Damon, a man of considerable influence in the city, to act as his go-between, and put a delicate question to the Japanese party: how would it be if he took Manjirō back to New Bedford, his hometown in America, and gave him a modern education?

Manjirō's friends were nonplussed. The five men had come drifting to these alien, distant shores together and to part with one of their countrymen now would be too painful. Even if they should never set foot on Japanese soil again, to forsake Manjirō, who was hardly more than a child, would be a beastly thing to do. Japan might be far away on the nether shore of a vast ocean, but didn't the old proverb say, "An evil deed can travel a thousand miles?" They might never see Tosa again, except when dreaming; but how could they ever face the people of Nakanohama and Nishihama, be it only in their dreams? On the other hand, the captain was their greatest benefactor, the man to whom they owed their lives. His compassion had made a deep imprint on their hearts. On top of that, he had negotiated with them through an important citizen of Honolulu, thus treating them with extraordinary courtesy. They pondered all this for some time, expressed a variety of opinions, and finally agreed that the decision should be left to Manjirō alone. Manjirō replied in a surprisingly lighthearted manner, "Well, if the captain wants me to cross over to America and breathe the air of civilization, so be it."

The captain was overjoyed when he heard of Manjirō's reply. "Don't worry about a thing," he assured his friends. "I'll take good care of him."

When he and Manjirō were boarding the ship, Denzō and the others came to see them off at the wharf, their hearts full of sadness at parting.

The government awarded Denzō's party the status of citizens on Oahu Island and gave them a small thatched cottage, about twelve feet by eighteen, to live in. Although the four Japanese felt a little crowded in the hut, it was an official donation and the men thanked the authorities for their generosity.

In those days the dwellings lining the streets of Honolulu were mostly cottages thatched with palm leaves: only the churches had real roofs, shaped like towers. There were no stone walls or donjons of the kind seen in Kōchi Castle, and the city generally couldn't be compared with the capital of the Tosa demesne.

But even in this late month its trees were thick with fresh green leaves. The harbor, almost a mile wide, faced south and there were never less than fifty whaling ships anchored there, the bright-starred American flag waving from their sterns.

Denzō and his men went on living at the government's expense until summer of the next year. They had become sufficiently acquainted with the language and customs to cope with simple errands, if not always to full satisfaction. But to depend on the government's support forever was humiliating, so they appealed to Governor George for some kind of work, anything to make them feel useful. The good doctor tried to set their minds at ease.

"Don't worry, you don't have any obligations. Just take it easy and keep drawing your allowance."

And so they spent another year living off the government, but the shame of being loafers, just idling away their time, was too hard to bear. They appealed to the governor once again. This time, Denzō and Goemon were given temporary jobs as servants in the doctor's mansion. They were asked to draw water, chop wood, deliver lunch-boxes, and clean up the house. Recommended by the governor, Toraemon became an apprentice to a cooper and moved into his house. Jūsuke, whose old foot sore was acting up again, was sent to a farm about six miles away from town to recuperate; his condition, however, seemed to be deteriorating.

4

Manjirō Enjoys the Thrill
of Deep-Sea Whaling

The *John Howland*, with Manjirō aboard, kept a steady southward course. The captain doted on the boy as if he were his own son and called him fondly "John Man," but one thing worried him: Manjirō couldn't read or write, and that might cause serious problems for him in the future. He encouraged Manjirō to study as much possible. As he practiced his letters, the boy soon realized that the alphabet with its twenty-six letters was shorter than the Japanese *iroha* which has forty-seven; it didn't take him long to master their spelling. The captain was very pleased and loved his "John Man" all the more. Soon the rest of the crew began calling him "John Man" too.

The ship called briefly at an island in the Kingsmill group, lying just below the equator, to store up on kindling and fresh water. It was a small island, a little over two miles in circumference. Its inhabitants were all black and wore nothing but tree leaves over their private parts, men and women alike. They came to the ship in their canoes to barter toy bows and arrows with the crew. The sailors traded useless pieces of scrap iron for the natives' ware, throwing them down into their boats.

The ship stayed in the waters around the Kingsmill Islands to hunt for whales, and in April 1842 sailed into a port on the Spanish island of Guam, lying due south of the Bonins. John Man went ashore with his American shipmates; the island was quite large, about eighty miles around, and its harbor at least ten miles in radius. Like the town houses of Honolulu, the houses here, numbering about three hundred, had thatched roofs.

Leaving Guam, the ship sailed due north, coasting a hundred to two hundred miles along Japanese shores toward the waters of Ishinomaki near Sendai. From there she turned south-southeast, down through the

Pacific Ocean, and landed on Eimeo Island, a British territory. This island too was about eighty miles in circumference, its three hundred huts covered with thatch like those of Guam and Honolulu. They had left Guam toward the end of May and arrived at Eimeo near the end of December. After spending about thirty days on Eimeo, they set sail for the southwest and, in March of the following year, again landed on Guam. The ship had roamed the entire Pacific west of Oahu, tracing a large circle in all four directions.

The *John Howland* lay at anchor in Guam for a month, then set sail for the south-southeast. By the end of May they had rounded Cape Horn at the tip of the South American continent and turned due north, and the next year [1844] saw them enter the port of New Bedford in the State of Massachusetts, U.S.A., at last. John Man had mastered the skills of whaling by now, as able a seaman as ever sailed the oceans.

New Bedford was a fine port about six miles wide and two miles deep, where two hundred whaling ships rode at anchor. The town seemed to have about five to six thousand houses. As soon as the ship entered port, a relief crew came out in a rowing boat, and the captain, John Man, and his shipmates took the boat back to shore. The town was densely populated, its streets amazingly busy. There was a gigantic bridge spanning a large river at least one mile wide. It was built as a drawbridge, so that even large ships could pass underneath with their masts erect. Accompanied by the captain, John Man crossed this bridge and arrived at the Whitfield residence in Fairhaven, lying on the other side of the river. The captain hadn't been home for fully five years.

Mrs. Whitfield had died of an illness during the captain's long absence, and his household now consisted of four people: his son, his daughter, a servant, and himself. From time to time, a farmhand was hired for temporary work.

The main street of Fairhaven ran along the seashore for two miles, and was lined with residential dwellings, most of them one- or two-storied structures with shingled roofs. John Man, who had never imagined such a splendid town could exist, was a little overwhelmed by its wonders at first. The captain's family called him "John Man" and treated him very kindly. Before long, the captain made arrangements for him to stay with the family of one James Allen, a cooper in the same town and a solid citizen of good common sense whose daughter Jane ran a private school a few blocks away from her father's house.

One day the cooper asked John Man if he wouldn't like to go to school and do some studying? "Oh yes, I'd like that very much," he replied. It seemed unlikely he'd be allowed to return to Japan for some time, he thought, and getting an education might come in handy.

But before going to school, he had first to acquire some basic knowledge. So Mr. Allen took him to his daughter's school and asked Miss Jane to give him reading practice.

Here John Man saw a "school" for the first time in his life: a wood-paneled room about thirty feet square where a score of students sat on benches behind rows of desks and practiced reading. The teacher stood on a wooden dais and wrote on the blackboard with a piece of white chalk.

Mr. Allen introduced John Man to his daughter. The pupils kept their distance from the new student at first, but in a few days started calling him "John Man," and before long he was a welcome companion in their games. Every morning John Man walked to school from the Allen house and didn't return until late afternoon. Once in a while, Miss Jane would lend him her reference materials.

Around that time, the captain took a trip to New York to sell his whale oil. Having made an excellent profit, he returned home in triumph, bringing along a beautiful new wife. Some farmland was bought about ten miles out of New Bedford, a new country house built on it, and the farm stocked with cows, pigs, and poultry. The surrounding fields were planted with crops, and some cultivated as a vineyard.

John Man took leave of Miss Jane's school and joined the captain's new household, ready to do his share of work. In his spare time, when there was no work in the fields or at the stables, John Man read his books. The captain had known the boy's love of learning from the beginning and admired him for it, but there was a mathematician by the name of Bartlett living in the neighborhood, who thought it especially laudable that a youth from such a far-off land should be so fond of learning. He offered to teach the boy some mathematics and surveying if he were willing. John Man wasted no time and gladly became Bartlett's pupil, studying arithmetic, surveying, reading, and penmanship under this scholar in his leisure moments. In November of the next year [1845] the captain embarked on another whaling expedition, sailing out of New Bedford. With the harvest in and the fieldwork completed for the season, John Man moved back to the cooper's house in the following March. Soon afterward he fell ill, however, and had to return to the Whitfield residence, where he took up his arithmetic with Mr. Bartlett once again. But he was a young man of twenty now and whenever he recalled the thrill of chasing whales in the great wide ocean, feeding pigs and poring over his sums became unbearably boring. How he yearned to sail the open seas again! It was just at this point that a sailor from New York by the name of Ira Davis came to see him, to ask if he'd like to join his whaling crew. This Davis had been a harpooner on the *John Howland*, the ship that had rescued John Man from the desert island, but he'd gone up in the world since then and was now the master of a New Bedford whaler called the *Franklin*. Davis had recognized his courage and fishing skills and was eager to hire him as a crew member for his new ship. To John Man, this was a godsend; obtaining the permission of the captain's wife in whose care he'd been left, he boarded the *Franklin*.

This ship was a three-master about a hundred and seventy feet long and had a crew of twenty-eight men. They weighed anchor in May 1846, called at Boston for two days and, setting their course due east, sailed out into the Atlantic. America was engaged in a war with Mexico then and the safest way to reach Pacific waters from the East Coast was to sail across the Atlantic.

The ship called briefly at the Farilhões Islands off the coast of Portugal, then took a southward course and passed close by the Canaries; refueling and getting water at a port on São Tiago in the Cape Verde Islands, they sailed around the southernmost tip of Africa and crossed the Indian Ocean. After some whaling in Australian waters and around Java, at the end of a seven-month voyage the *Franklin* at last reached Kupang on the island of Timor. Although the island itself belonged to the Portuguese, the port of Kupang was Dutch territory. It was a good harbor, lying at the end of a deep bay that ran about ten miles inland. John Man and the other sailors had thirty days to go ashore and inspect the town. The original inhabitants of the island were black, but lived together with the Dutch settlers and some East Indians; the number of houses was about two hundred.

This sea voyage truly opened John Man's eyes. He saw every kind of clime and landscape, met people of every race and color. After they had weighed anchor from Kupang, they called briefly at New Guinea. There he saw a race of cannibals who dyed their heads white and smeared their faces with mud; John Man could hardly tell the males from the females. His shipmates were eager to obtain some native shields and weapons, but this involved a fair amount of danger and the idea had to be abandoned.

The ship then landed on one of the islands of the Doron group lying north of Borneo to restock her supply of fuel and water. The *Franklin* lay at anchor here for thirty days while the crew had a good rest. She then sailed out again toward the East China Sea, hunting whales along the way, passed the coast of Taiwan, and reached the Ryūkyū Islands. John Man had kept handy a set of Japanese kimono and a white headband for just such an occasion, but for once courage failed him and he missed his opportunity to go ashore. Some of the men lowered a boat and rowed out to a seaside hamlet where they bartered four rolls of calico for two cows—a very bad bargain for the Ryūkyū villagers, given the standard price of commodities. The men also talked about getting hold of some tangerines and fresh pork, but finally agreed that any further violation of Japanese seclusion laws might be unwise and put to sea in a hurry. Now the ship's course was set for the east, toward the desert island where John Man and his shipmates had once been stranded. They caught some whales in its vicinity and a fair amount of fish for the ship's kitchen. In October of the same year, when they were sailing about a hundred and sixty miles off the coast of northern Japan, they ran into a fleet of about twenty Japanese fishing boats. A great school of bonito had gathered here, and the men on the Japanese boats were pulling them out in a dizzying flurry of activity; even the ocean around seemed to have taken on the color of fish. The *Franklin*'s crew also wanted a share in this bounty. Lowering the ship's sails, every sailor took out his fishing gear and started hauling in the bonito.

When they had hooked about two hundred of them, two of the Japanese boats rowed over to the *Franklin*, thinking perhaps the foreign ship was encroaching on their fishing grounds, or simply that her behavior was suspicious. Rising to the occasion, John Man changed into his kimono and wrapped the headband around his forehead in the Japanese style. Then he stood by the bulwark and called out to the boats as loudly as he could:

"Where do you come from? Japanese boats, I take it. Where is your home port?"

After so many years, John Man was speaking Japanese again. No more in a dream, but in real life now, he called in his mother tongue as loudly as he pleased to fellow countrymen of his.

"What part of Japan do your boats come from? Are they from Tosa?"

"Sentei, Sentei," came the answer from the boats. Most probably it was the word Sendai, spoken in their local brogue. John Man had a boat launched at once, took two baskets of bread as a present, and rowed over to the fishing boats from "Sentei." Bringing his gunwale alongside one of their hulls, he passed the bread baskets to the fishermen. They accepted the present and opened the lids, but looked at the contents with suspicion. John Man spoke to a sturdy-looking youngster, who seemed to be the leader of the fishing party from "Sentei."

"Are your boats going back to Tosa?"

The sturdy young man looked puzzled, as if he couldn't understand his Tosa accent: "Don't know."

"Well then, do you know if there is a boat that's going back to Tosa?"

The young man again replied, "Don't know."

"Can't you understand what I'm saying? Just tell me if any of your boats are going back to Tosa!"

The young fisherman gave the same answer as before: "Don't know."

Then he picked up one of the bonito they'd caught and tried to hand it over as a return present, saying "*Katsuo*." Obviously afraid they might get into trouble, these men pretended not to understand a word of what John Man was saying. John Man gave up further attempts at verbal communication and simply gestured to them, "We've also caught plenty of *katsuo*. Thanks for your present, but I trust you won't get angry if I refuse it." Realizing that further questioning would be useless, he rowed back to the ship. The captain and the crew had been watching his conference with the Japanese fishermen from the deck, all well aware how painfully homesick John Man was for his Tosa. When he reached the ship, his disappointment grew even worse, and he forgot to take off his headband until someone reminded him. Had there been a ship going to Tosa, he would have negotiated with Captain Davis and tried to enter his country illegally. From there the *Franklin* set course for the southeast and continued her cruise, running with amazing speed before favorable winds. By December she had entered the port of Honolulu on Oahu Island where it was decided that the ship would rest for a while and replenish her supplies of fuel and water.

More than six years had passed since John Man bade farewell to Denzō and his other friends on this wharf. He could hardly wait for his leave, and as soon as the captain gave the word he rushed ashore. He inquired about the whereabouts of his countrymen from an office clerk and a tailor he used to know, but was told that Denzō and his son had gone home to Japan, Jūsuke had fallen ill and died, and only Toraemon was still in town, serving as an apprentice to a local carpenter. When Manjirō arrived at the carpenter's house, Toraemon was cutting a piece of lumber with a huge saw, as vigorous as ever. He was so astounded to see Manjirō he could only mumble, "Oh, it's Manjirō-san!"

"I never expected to see you again," he went on in English. "How wonderful to meet you! When did you come?"

"Tora-san!" exclaimed Manjirō, but he too went on in English. "Yes, isn't it wonderful. And what a pleasure to see you looking so well. I landed here a couple of days ago on the *Franklin*, and learned that you were staying at this workshop. I also heard that Den-san and Goemon had gone back to Japan, and that poor Jūsuke wasn't with us any more."

"Yes, poor man. We felt so sorry for him. He breathed his last, repeating 'I'm going home to Japan at least in spirit.' I remember it was on a windy day in February last year. Den-san and Goemon had left for Japan on the *Florida* toward the end of November. I was hoping to join them, but then changed my mind, as the captain of the *Florida*, Mr. Cox, is a crooked man. It's much harder to put up with pain and suffering on a long sea voyage, I felt. But enough of my talk, let me hear what you've been doing since you left."

John Man began to talk about his own experiences, the whole long story of those six years, from his trip to America with Captain Whitfield to his last job on the whaling ship and her recent cruise that brought him here and provided this rare chance to meet. They were still busy comparing notes, when another carpenter, one of Toraemon's mates, happened by.

"Toraemon! I just met a sailor from a whaling ship at the chandler's in the harbor. He claims that the *Florida* has made port with your old friend Denzō on board. I guess that proves what you've been saying all along—the captain of the *Florida* is obviously a crook."

The news left John Man and Toraemon aghast. They ran to the harbor where they found the *Florida* at anchor. Renting a boat, they rowed over to the ship and, sure enough, Denzō and his son were both aboard.

5

Denzō and His Son Fail to Land
in Japan and Sail Back to Hawaii

Denzō now accounted for his own adventures during the six years since they had parted.

He told John Man how they'd found shelter and care at Dr. George the governor's mansion, but how even that became depressing in time so they had to rent a cottage to be able to stand on their own feet. With no experience in business, nor any capital to buy land, they managed to make a living as coolies or farmhands during harvest time. Jūsuke had taken ill with dysentery three years before, around August or September, and though neighbors did their best for him, he died in February of the previous year. Denzō had a Christian priest read prayers for him and interred his remains in the burial plot of Jūsuke's former master, putting up a wooden tablet to mark the grave. Denzō became so dejected after his younger brother's death that a man called Tuwana had to take care of him and Goemon. Once, when the king of the islands came to Oahu on a royal tour, he chanced to pay a visit to Tuwana's house. There he received Denzō and his son in audience and inquired about their recent past. Denzō recounted the various circumstances of their stay on the islands in great detail, and expressed their wish for an independent living as farmers and part-time fishermen. Several days after the king's visit, Tuwana summoned Denzō and his son and announced, "You've been awarded some land!"

The king must have granted their wish and ordered Tuwana to make the necessary arrangements.

So Denzō and Goemon built a cottage on some vacant land near the beach and went about their fishing and farming. They made themselves fishing tackle just like the kind they'd used back home in Tosa, casting mainly for bonito and selling their catch at city markets. Skilled in the art of bonito fishing since childhood, Denzō could hook fifty before a native islander got ten. They planted potatoes in the fields they now owned; the weather was good, and they had a bumper crop. Being exempt from all taxes, they were able to lead a comfortable life, if not exactly one of luxury. When Goemon had nothing to do in the fields, he'd go and help out in the home of a missionary he knew. Denzō followed the custom of the natives and farmers of the island and kept chickens and pigs for their table.

One day when the missionary was giving a sermon at his home, Goemon heard a voice calling him from the congregation.

"Goemon, Goemon. Have you forgotten me?"

He looked closer, and saw it was Captain Whitfield of the *Howland*. The captain asked with a broad smile: "Don't you remember me?"

Could Goemon have forgotten a man to whom he owed his life?

"Of course I remember you. How could I forget the man who saved our lives? Your kindness, Captain, will always remain in our hearts."

The captain smiled again warmly and asked about Goemon's father and the others. When he heard that Jūsuke had died, his face clouded with grief.

"I'm here to tell you that I'm taking steps to send you back to Japan," he said. "I had a sailor by the name of Cox on the *Howland* who's become the master of his own whaler; he's about to leave for Japanese waters and I thought we might use the opportunity to provide passage for all of you. I'm sorry Jūsuke is dead—I can imagine how he would have loved to go back home. Well, there's nothing we can do. But the three of you had better make use of this chance. I'll ask Mr. Cox to look after you. By the way, Manjirō is living happily in my hometown, so you needn't worry about him. Just run back home and start packing."

The captain followed Goemon to the seaside cottage, to pay his father a visit.

Denzō's house was so poor that Captain Whitfield kept frowning when he was shown inside. There were no chairs to sit on and hardly any room to stand, and Denzō had to bring in a barrel so that their benefactor could at least sit down. The captain seated himself on the barrel, still frowning. Then he looked out at the ocean and laughed.

"Well, there's nothing like simple country living!"

Whitfield explained about the ship bound for Japan and told them to come to the harbor in the morning to talk the matter over. Before he left the cottage, he gave them two silver pieces.

The next day, when Goemon appeared on the quay, the captain looked at his clothes. "I'm afraid you can't go back to Japan dressed like that. You'd better put these on," he said, handing him a woolen suit, a pair of shoes, a hat, and a few undershirts. Goemon packed all these items into a bundle, slung it on a pole over his shoulder, and returned to their cottage.

Denzō and Goemon were so happy they had to rush to Honolulu and break the news to Toraemon.

"Tora-san, we've got something to tell you!" and they explained all the details, vowing to return to Japan together.

The three men went the rounds of their best friends in Honolulu to say goodbye. When they came to bid farewell to the governor, Dr. George gave them some money, clothing, and other parting presents. Most of their close friends listened to their farewell address with tears in their eyes.

Returning to the cottage from Honolulu, Denzō and Goemon started getting ready for departure. To part with the fields where they had toiled so hard wasn't easy, but the joy of going home was worth any sacrifice. They offered the potatoes and millet from their fields to the neighbors and returned the land to the donor's agent, Tuwana. The six chickens, four ducks, and two pigs they had kept were presented to Captain Whitfield.

The captain introduced Denzō and his men to Mr. Cox, skipper of the *Florida*, asking him to take good care of them. When they were boarding the ship—a whaler with a crew of twenty-five—Captain Whitfield came to see them off. But just when the ship was ready to sail, Toraemon changed his mind.

"I'm not going back. And I have good reasons."

Much surprised, Denzō did his best to persuade him that if he didn't return home then, he might never be able to. But Toraemon kept saying that the voyage would be unlucky as long as "that blackhearted man" was aboard. He must have had serious doubts about Captain Cox's character. No matter how much they pressed him, he stubbornly refused to listen and at last went back ashore all by himself.

The *Florida* left Honolulu before the end of November. Taking a southward course, she did some whale hunting in the waters of the South Seas and put in at Guam to welcome the New Year. From there she headed north and by mid-April had reached the vicinity of Hachijō Island, but the seas were too rough to launch a boat. Passing about three leagues off the island, the *Florida* headed northeast and sailed along the coast of the Bōsō Peninsula. By mid-May she was whaling off the Matsumae coast, coming so close to the mainland that they could see its dim outline. Captain Cox told Denzō that the cape in sight was part of Matsumae and brought the ship to within a league and a half of the coast. A boat was lowered into the water and the captain, Denzō, Goemon, and six oarsmen took it ashore, landing on the north side. Wandering around for a while in search of some habitation, they discovered two small vacant houses of about nine by twelve feet each. Inside they found two kinds of straw sandals, *zōri* and *waraji*, and a straw raincoat, hanging from the wall. On the earthen floor lay a pair of worn-out *waraji*, as if kicked off in a hurry. But the traces of soil on them looked white and dry, and the ashes in the hearth were dead and cold. In spite of themselves, Denzō and Goemon shouted, "Hey, anybody home?" but there was no answer, not even an echo. When they looked behind the house, they found a field planted with taro. There was no doubt they were on Japanese territory, but hard as they searched the area, not a living soul could be found. They even climbed a small hill nearby and made a bonfire, waiting for a long while, but no one showed up.

"The island's deserted," the captain said. "You'd just be making things harder for yourselves if you went ashore here. Let's go back to the ship— I'll find you a better place to land."

Go back, after all the trouble they had taken to land here? No matter what hardships lay ahead, Denzō and his son had to find a human dwelling and fulfill their long-cherished desire to return home. They begged Cox to leave them behind, but the captain ignored their pleas.

"What would I say to Mr. Whitfield if I left you marooned on a desert island like this? We'll have plenty of opportunities to put you ashore in a more suitable place than this desolate corner of the earth."

But Denzō and Goemon were resolved to stay at any cost and endure any amount of hardship. Still the captain wouldn't hear of it. So they clasped their hands above their heads and implored him:

"Captain, we've never asked you for anything and never will again. Just this one wish, for pity's sake: leave us here!"

"Sorry, I can't" was the captain's curt and final reply. The two men returned to the ship in a wretched mood.

Keeping to a steady northern course, the *Florida* sailed toward the Aleutian Islands and caught more whales in Arctic waters. By mid-September she had harvested twenty-three of them and was ready to start her homeward run for Honolulu; it took another forty sunless days before they left the gloomy Arctic seas behind.

Having recounted the long story of their wandering, Denzō added that it was on this very day they had returned to Honolulu. John Man, who had listened intently to Denzō's words, put in:

"I don't think Cox is as black as Toraemon here paints him."

"Oh, he's blackhearted enough for me," said Toraemon, not bending in his opinion.

Judging from the practical results of the matter, it did look as if Cox had tricked them into boarding the *Florida*, just as Toraemon had been warning from the beginning. That way he could employ two extra men on the whaling crew, and they cost him nothing. On the other hand, Cox knew about Japan's seclusion policies and had risked grave danger when he led the landing party to the coast of Matsumae. He had personally helped them look for human habitation, even climbing a hill to light a bonfire. Wouldn't it be fair to say he hadn't dared desert them out of respect for his former master, Captain Whitfield?

But John Man's ship, the *Franklin*, was about to sail any minute and he had to break off the long conversation, saying goodbye and "until we meet again" to his friends.

Denzō and Goemon went the rounds of their former friends once again. Calling on every house where they had received parting presents when they were leaving for Japan, they reported how their hopes had ended in failure, and asked for their friends' continued support and goodwill. Then they moved to a place called Maeha, about ten miles from Honolulu, and settled down as common peasants.

6
John Man Sails Back to America and Honolulu

From Honolulu the *Franklin* set out on a cruise of the South Seas, and in April 1848 she anchored at Guam to restock on fuel and water. John Man had been here before, but his docking turned out to be no routine one: all of a sudden, their captain, Ira Davis, started acting so violently there was little doubt that he was going mad. A meeting of the entire crew was called at once and it was decided to take him to Manila on Luzon Island. They sailed into Manila harbor in late June, after doing some whaling on the way.

There was an American consulate in Manila, and some crew members asked for a hearing with the consul, explaining the matter to him. They arranged to have the captain repatriated to the States on a government ship. Because of this affair, John Man had ample opportunity to spend time ashore. With a smart new hat on his head, he strolled around the town, where people of all nations mingled together. Besides Americans, there were Spaniards, Dutchmen, Englishmen, Indians, and Chinese—a veritable emporium of human races.

Since the *Franklin* had no skipper now, Mr. Miller, the first officer, was appointed acting captain, and by the unanimous vote of the crew John Man was chosen to serve as his deputy. The sailors had all come to respect their Japanese mate's courage and whaling skills.

In August, the *Franklin* left Manila to hunt for whales in the waters around the Batan Islands, Taiwan, and the Ryūkyūs, and in November again made port in Guam. Refilling her supplies of food and water here, she weighed anchor in December and sailed toward New Ireland, touching at Celebes in March of the next year. In April, she rounded the island of Timor and put in at Seram. While the ship lay at anchor here for some twenty days, John Man bought a parrot on one of his excursions ashore and took it back to the ship.

The island of Seram lies north of Australia, near Timor. From here the *Franklin* sailed southwest through the Indian Ocean, passed Madagascar in July, and rounding the Cape of Good Hope went straight north into the Atlantic. By October, they finally reached their home port of New Bedford, which they had last seen three years ago in May 1846. On its grand sea voyage, the *Franklin* had circumnavigated the globe, taking a bounty of five hundred whales. The expedition yielded several thousand barrels of whale oil.

John Man collected his share of the profits (about $350) and returned to his second home, the Whitfield residence in Fairhaven. He learned that the captain had also completed a voyage just a few days before, and was already waiting for him. John Man was a little worried that the captain might scold him for running off during his absence, but there wasn't a word of reproach. On the contrary, Mr. Whitfield warmly congratulated him on the success of the whaling expedition and his promotion to second in command of the *Franklin*. John Man told the captain about his chance encounter with Denzō in Honolulu, and Denzō's sad story, but the captain said that the Matsumae shore where Denzō's party had landed was most probably not part of the mainland. The ocean northeast of Matsumae was dotted with islands running out like stepping-stones, and on some you could see cottages built by Japanese settlers. What Denzō's party found must have been such houses. And so, the captain concluded, Mr. Cox's decision was the right one after all.

Captain Whitfield was thoroughly familiar with the shape of the Japanese coast, and on a recent voyage had even rowed a boat into the offing near Edo to inspect Edo Bay in detail. He had also picked up some shipwrecked Japanese sailors, who offered him a handful of Japanese coins as a token of their gratitude.

"Here," he said producing about twenty coins with square holes in the center and offering them to John Man. "These are your country's coins, aren't they? They'll be of more value to you than to me." He explained that he'd had thirty or forty of them, but he'd given one or two away to each of his neighbors, who appreciated their rarity. Most of the people of Fairhaven had a taste for curios, and they set great store on

Japanese artifacts. One of the town's wealthiest men kept a prized collection of Japanese swords, straw sandals, and *tabi* socks. There were people who displayed miniature models of Japanese portable shrines on the mantelpieces of their parlors. Most of these objects had been acquired from Dutch ships they had met at sea.

John Man was staying with the Whitfields again when a major event that was to shake the very economic foundations of the North American continent occurred: an immense deposit of nuggets and gold dust was discovered in California.

Thus began the age of the Gold Rush, and soon dreams of gold had sent thousands of people flocking to California. Like everybody else, John Man was infected by this gold fever. He had decided to go back to Japan anyhow, and California was on his way. To Captain Whitfield he only said he was going south to dig for gold, keeping his desire to return home a secret. Otherwise, the captain would surely have put him under house arrest.

John Man reached California via South America, hired as a deckhand on a New Bedford lumber ship. Not only could he save expenses this way, a sea route was also the safest way to travel in those days. Arriving in California, he went upriver from Sacramento, set up camp in one of the mining settlements, and started prospecting for gold.

The first forty days he worked under a Dutch miner who contracted him for a daily wage of six silver pieces, but the man was a born swindler. California had become a meeting place for notorious scoundrels from all over the world and the Dutchman, apparently one of the local gang bosses, was no exception. Although John Man demanded his wages, the Dutchman found all kinds of excuses and never paid him a cent. He tried to work on his own for about a month, but his health failed him and he had to give up prospecting and return to San Francisco.

Still, that last month yielded a profit of 270 silver pieces and a handful of nuggets: a fair sum, but not enough to outfit a boat that would carry them back to Japan. Anyway, he'd first have to sail back to Honolulu, meet with Denzō and the others, and make proper plans.

Again he worked for his passage, this time on a merchant vessel bound directly for Honolulu, and earned his sailor's wages into the bargain.

When he landed in Honolulu, John Man went to see Toraemon and sent for Denzō and his son, who were working as farmers in Maeha. They both came to see him at once. The four men sat down for a conference, trying to work out a plan for their trip home, but there was one serious obstacle. Denzō's son Goemon had been converted to the foreigners' religion and a friend had introduced him to a young woman whom he'd married. She was a good and virtuous girl and their married life was very happy.

No wonder Goemon was thunderstruck when he heard about their plans. To run away from a good wife would never do, and yet if he missed this opportunity he might never set foot on Japanese soil again—a sad, sad situation. His conversion to the foreign religion could easily be kept secret from Japanese officials, but to take an alien female back to Japan was out of the question.

Denzō pondered his son's predicament with a heavy heart. He couldn't ask him to abandon a good wife. Then again, he couldn't leave his only son behind in a foreign land either. For his part, he was determined not to let this opportunity pass.

To keep their plans secret, they did all their talking in Japanese.

"I don't know right from wrong any more," said Denzō. "It's like in that old Tosa saying about letting the devil into your heart."

He looked at his son's face, and saw it turn pale. He spoke to John Man and Toraemon. "Believe me, Tora-san and Manjirō-san, the only thing that's kept me alive till now is the thought of going back to Japan."

Both Toraemon and John Man nodded forcefully, but they said nothing. The long silence was at last broken by Goemon.

"All right, I'll go."

It was decided that he should sneak on board without letting his wife know.

That day, a rumor reached them that a ship carrying some Japanese passengers had entered Honolulu harbor. John Man hurried to the quay and visited the ship, but when he met the Japanese party, he found he couldn't understand a word of their Japanese. So he sent for Denzō, who interviewed them. The newcomers, it turned out, were skipper Torakichi and his five crewmen from the *Tenju maru*, a tangerine boat from Hidaka in the province of Kii. Driven by a typhoon, they had drifted on the open sea until rescued by a foreign ship and brought to this harbor. Denzō and his men had often seen Kii boats in the waters of their homeland, and were pleased to hear that these men came from a place so near Tosa. They promised each other they would return to Japan together. Denzō and his friends were happy to have found fellow travelers. But once again Toraemon had a change of heart, saying that he'd rather stay behind by himself. He explained that since he already had so many friends and acquaintances in town it really made little difference whether he spent the rest of his life here or in Tosa. Denzō and John Man could hardly believe their ears. To leave one of their countrymen behind alone? They tried their best to bring him to his senses. "How can we ever explain it to the people at home," they pleaded, "if we leave you behind?"

Yet no matter how forcefully they argued, Toraemon wouldn't listen. He just kept saying, "Your last plan to return ended in failure, and so will this one." Toraemon was making a decent living as a cooper in Honolulu, and he was probably too young to feel the ache of home-sickness as urgently as an older man would.

The three men decided to return without Toraemon, but couldn't avoid some ill feeling toward him. They were allowed to board the American vessel with the shipwrecked crew from Kii, but John Man and the captain soon got embroiled in a quarrel and his party had to leave the ship. Several days before she was scheduled to sail, John Man, find-ing time heavy on his hands, had started fixing some broken barrels. When the captain saw his work, he ordered him to mend some more of them. When all the barrels were done, the captain had all kinds of tools and articles of furniture brought out and piled high on deck.

"You fix these things real quick, and that's an order!"

"I'm sorry, but I can't," replied John Man, who had some skill as a cooper but knew nothing about mechanical repairs and carpentry.

Without another word, the captain slapped him hard in the face. John Man was furious—it was only slaves who received this sort of treatment in America.

"I'm not a slave. Remember a seaman's honor!—instead of strutting around with that clay pipe sticking out of your face."

Spitting out his anger, John Man turned his back on the captain's boxes and chairs and didn't touch a thing. The captain, no less incensed, tried to force his will on the three men, but John Man and his friends decided

107

to postpone their trip home until the next opportunity. Full of bitterness, they left the ship when it was almost ready to sail. Torakichi of the Kii crew, a kind and gentle man, kept repeating in a voice brimming with sympathy:

"I can't tell you how sorry we feel for you. . . ."

From the wharf the three men went to see their friend Toraemon, the cooper. He laughed at them, as much as to say "Serves you right," but then frowned and said, "There's been trouble." Yesterday, and for about four or five days before that, Goemon's wife had come to his place to make urgent inquiries about her husband.

"Where is Goemon, Tora-san? You must know!" Toraemon kept answering "I don't know, I've no idea."

True to the secret agreement with his comrades, Goemon hadn't told her anything, preferring to sneak out of the house without a word. A good and virtuous wife she might be, but this time she was bound to throw a tantrum. The rumor that once again their plans to be repatriated had gone awry would soon reach the ear of the public throughout Honolulu. Even worse, it might appear in the newspapers. The *Polynesian* and *Friend* were always eager to outdo one another by printing such stories.

Denzō and Goemon went back to their homestead in Maeha. They slipped into the house quietly, like a couple of mice. There, under the picture of Christ on the wall, the young wife was kneeling, absorbed in prayer. Noticing that someone had come into the house, she looked up in surprise and jumped to her feet. Seeing it was Goemon, she let out a wild shriek and dashed over, clinging fast to his shoulder. Overcome with joy, she made no scene—just embraced him and pressed her lips to his. Denzō had seen her acting like this before, more often than he cared; this time he simply picked up his old hoe from the earthen floor and went straight out to work in the field.

Goemon's wife was indeed a good woman. While they were away, she had tilled the one-acre farm and built a duck shed in a corner of the field. She had already managed to install a pair of ducks in their new home. This woman must really enjoy farming, Denzō thought.

John Man waited for another chance to go home, doing miscellaneous jobs for the ships anchored in Honolulu harbor. He asked all his old friends in the city to help them find a suitable ship, and soon learned through the grapevine that there was a merchant vessel bound for Shanghai. She was an American freighter called the *Sarah Boyd* and had docked there in early December of 1850 on her way to pick up a cargo of Chinese tea. John Man took the good news to Denzō and Goemon, and the three of them went to see Captain Fitzmore of the *Sarah Boyd*, showing him their identity cards issued by the American consul.

When John Man told the captain their story and asked his leave to sail on the *Sarah Boyd*, the captain looked rather reluctant.

"I can imagine how you men must be longing to return to your country. But a ship that sails to Shanghai passes far south of Japan. A merchantman isn't a whaler—she has to keep to a strict schedule. To change her course at whim in order to approach a Japanese port is out of the question. You see, the *Sarah Boyd* is owned by a shipping company, and the merchants to whom we deliver her cargo of tea think no shipment is too early. There's no way I could act on my own authority and change the ship's course."

Despite his words, the captain seemed moved by their passionate longing for home. He spread a chart before them and explained:

"Look, here is China and Shanghai, and here is Satsuma in Japan. When the wind is fair, our ship sometimes passes through the coastal waters of Satsuma. There might be a way to land a boat on one of the islands nearby. But I can't promise you anything—it all depends on favorable winds."

John Man and the other two put their heads together, trying to decide what to do. If the winds weren't favorable, they'd have to sail on to Shanghai, and then back to Honolulu again. Yet if they missed this chance, there was no way of knowing when another would present itself.

"Let's board this boat and find a way to get back home," they concluded and John Man came up with a plan: "We'll buy and outfit a small rowing boat, stowing it aboard the *Sarah Boyd*. As soon as we reach Japanese coastal waters, we'll put it over the side and try to row ashore."

Denzō and Goemon thought it was a wonderful idea and seconded it at once. Even Captain Fitzmore found it practical and said to John Man with a smile: "You've really given it some thought, haven't you?"

From the *Sarah Boyd* the three men went directly to Toraemon's place and begged him once again to join them. But Toraemon wouldn't hear of it, saying that crossing a stretch of open sea in a small rowing boat was too dangerous. Obviously he had lost much of his fervor to go back to Japan.

John Man ran busily all around town to see if anyone would sell him a small boat. Although he had hoarded his silver coins and gold dust from California as if his life depended on it, a new boat was beyond his means and he had to look for a used one. As luck would have it, he heard that some Englishman was willing to part with a boat and all the necessary tackle for a hundred dollars.

He christened his craft the *Adventure* and took it aboard the *Sarah Boyd*. Their own boarding time was coming close, too. Many of Honolulu's citizens had heard the rumor about these desperate seafarers, and went out of their way to help them get ready for the voyage. Samuel Damon appealed to the public in a daily paper on their behalf and raised substantial funds for them. The *Polynesian* printed the following notice on December 17, 1850.

> John Manjirō, a member of the shipwrecked crew of Japanese who were rescued by Captain Whitfield in 1841, was given an elementary education in the States by Mr. Whitfield. Mr. Manjirō, who also managed to acquire a cooper's skills, now contemplates returning to Japan with two other countrymen of his. They plan to sail on the *Sarah Boyd*, an American freighter bound for China, from Mazatlan in Mexico, having reached an agreement with the captain, Mr. Fitzmore, to be delivered to the vicinity of the Ryūkyū Islands. They need a whaleboat and some tackle to accomplish their risky scheme. Charitable citizens are kindly requested to contribute the following items: a mariner's compass, rifles, clothes, boots, and a nautical almanac for 1850.

The moment Goemon's wife saw this ad, she knew that her husband was going back to Japan and she was heartbroken. But she had come to understand how singleminded the Japanese can be and simply said to him, "I'll always wait for you, no matter what."

John Man wrote to his benefactor, Captain Whitfield, expressing his gratitude for the American's unusual kindness over the past many years.

He also apologized for leaving the captain's home for good without his permission or a word of farewell. Finally, he asked the captain to give away his personal belongings to friends and dispatched the letter by a ship bound for America.

Once again the three Japanese went the rounds of their many friends. But as the ship was about to sail any minute, they had to cut the leave-taking short and go aboard in a sad, unresolved mood.

7

Home at Last: John Man and His Mates Make Successful Landfall in the Ryūkyūs

The *Sarah Boyd*, a vessel of some hundred and twenty feet and a crew of seventeen, left Oahu on December 28, but the winds were unfavorable and she was unable to keep the plotted course. When they finally reached a point less than two leagues off the coast of the Ryūkyūs on the second day of the Japanese New Year, after forty long days of cruising, John Man and his mates felt a great surge of joy. He wanted to share this joy with their friends in Oahu and wrote to one of them on the spot, asking him to urge Toraemon to follow their example. He entrusted the letter to the captain's care.

They thanked the captain for giving them passage and, although the seas were rough, got ready to lower their *Adventure* into the stormy water. The captain brought the ship to and shook each man's hand.

"This will be a risky landing, men," he said, his eyes wet with tears. "I'm afraid the sea might be a bit too choppy to row ashore. Come back to the ship if you fail to make it. And don't take too many chances."

Then he added, as a last farewell, "They say the laws of your country are strict; I'm afraid I may never see you again. Goodbye to you, and the best of luck to the *Adventure!*"

The three men bade farewell to the captain and called "*Sayōnara, sayōnara*" to the crew. The boat went over the side; they boarded it and rowed toward the shadowy island over the heaving waves. When the crew of the *Sarah Boyd* saw they had safely reached the island, they hoisted full sail and the ship soon disappeared in a westerly direction.

The three Japanese brought the boat close to the rocky shore, but the wind and rain lashing at them wouldn't let them land. It was getting dark. That night, they moored the boat in the lee of a cliff and waited for dawn, tossed by the waves. The boat was laden with their personal effects and presents, food, and other goods, but it was of a sturdy design made to resist the heaviest breakers, and there was no danger of capsizing.

At daybreak the next day, the third after New Year's, the wind and rain stopped. On the shore beyond the coastline, they could see some farmhouses with tangerine trees in their gardens. They rowed the *Adventure* to the beach and Denzō went ashore by himself to reconnoiter. Of the three, he was the one who had best retained his Japanese. But when he entered one of the cottages and asked the name of the village, the peasant family inside were so startled by his outlandish costume that their peaceful New-Year's-week breakfast ended in bedlam. Chattering among themselves, they left their table in panic, ready to run away from the house. Denzō kept explaining that he meant absolutely no harm, but they couldn't understand his Tosa dialect any better than he could their local brogue. He had no other course than to run back to the boat and report to John Man.

"They don't understand me at all. Maybe I've forgotten my Japanese during the long stay abroad."

John Man secured the boat on shore, put a pistol in his pocket for protection, and headed toward the village. Denzō and Goemon followed him. He met a villager on the road, but since they couldn't understand each other, he made gestures of drinking with cupped hands and the man led them to a well. They fetched their supplies and kitchen tools from the boat and cooked some beef and pork, their first meal since the night before. While they were taking their after-dinner rest and drinking coffee, a group of villagers came by and gestured that they should follow them to a ramshackle shed, probably a watchman's shelter. The natives apparently took them for castaways from a foreign land.

Yet the people of this island knew how to treat castaways. Some of them were kind enough to bring drinking water, others brought sweet potatoes. Someone even gave them a measure of rice. In the meantime, a village official must have been notified, for he arrived in the company of a host of village clerks. The official's language was a little different from the local dialect and they could make out some words.

The official questioned John Man and his men as to their nationality, their names, their port of departure as well as their destination, and checked all their possessions. Then he confiscated John Man's pistol, ruling that they would have to be escorted to a Village Office for further investigation. This village, they learned, was called Mabunimagiri and lay near the southernmost tip of Okinawa Island in the Ryūkyūs.

They were escorted to the Village Office of a place called Nakao. The heavily armed attendants never took their eyes off them, but Denzō, who had developed some eye trouble, was allowed to ride in a litter most of the way. Though the escort's treatment of John Man's party was not exactly cruel, they still couldn't quite believe that these three ragamuffins in barbarians' clothing were real Japanese, and everybody's nerves were on edge throughout the trip.

From the village of Mabunimagiri to Nakao was about four miles. The three men were first accommodated in the house of a peasant by the name of Peichin, and the same evening summoned to the official's quarters, where they were interrogated late into the night. They had trouble understanding the official and he them, so they had to be summoned for continued interrogation the next morning. But the two cross-examinations at least convinced the official that the men were true Japanese. The peasant in whose house they were quartered, Peichin, also testified that his castaways took their steamed rice with chopsticks and therefore had to be Japanese. Of course, the officials had no way of telling to what extent the castaways' minds had been exposed to dangerous ideas, or how much foreign "civilization" had seeped in.

On the last day of the New Year's festive fortnight, the fourteenth, they were again summoned to the Village Office. This time a more senior-looking official had come from Satsuma. With three lower clerks acting as witnesses, he thoroughly examined all the castaways' personal belongings, their luggage and books. The books in particular were subjected to a careful scrutiny by the presiding official who turned page after page with growing curiosity. Staring at the geometrical diagrams in the textbook of surveying, he seemed to be wondering: these suspicious charts look like secret ciphers, don't they? The witnessing clerks, who inspected the charts in their turn, obviously thought the textbooks no more than a lot of nonsense. They whispered to each other that the circles—actually drawings with bow compasses—looked very like the pictures foreign children drew on the ground when they played. But the Satsuma official reproved them.

114

"No, these must be illustrations to some kind of profound learning!"

Though a senior official of the Satsuma clan, Ogawa Shōnosuke was a good-natured young samurai. He told the village officials to be kind to the castaways and advised John Man that under no circumstances was he to lose his temper. Only last year, a shipwrecked Sendai boatman by the name of Sajūrō who'd returned from Russia had become so exasperated by the severity of his interrogation that he flew into a rage and eventually committed suicide. But the lord of Satsuma would never treat Japanese castaways in such a harsh way, Ogawa assured John Man. The interrogation they were going through now might appear strict, but it was after all nothing but a formality prescribed by the law before they were handed over to the high commissioner of Nagasaki, who stood directly under Tokugawa jurisdiction. John Man and the others felt encouraged by this and thanked Ogawa for his kindness. Of course they wouldn't have dreamed that the call "Down with the Tokugawa government" was ringing throughout Satsuma just then.

They were still kept in custody at Peichin's house as ordered by the Satsuma official, constantly watched by shifts of the five Satsuma clerks and two Ryūkyū officials. But their treatment left nothing to be desired. The food bill was shouldered by the local government, and Peichin was able to serve them a varied and plentiful fare of pork, chicken, fish, eggs, and tōfu. Their clothing was donated by the tribal king of the Ryūkyūs, and consisted of Japanese *haori* coats and *hakama* skirts. As hot summer days were soon to follow, they were given some mosquito nets, light summer kimono, sashes, and loincloths. Once in a while, a bottle of Ryūkyū *awamori*—a sweet-potato brandy—came their way.

This kind of life lasted for seven months, till the eighteenth of the Seventh Month, when they were transferred again. Guarded by their official escort, the three men were put into litters and their American articles distributed among local porters. They left Peichin's house in the evening, and their host, obviously sorry to see them go, came to see them off to the very outskirts of the village. It was too dark to make out the lie of the land along the roadside. As soon as they arrived in Naha, the capital of the Ryūkyūs, they were taken to a waiting ship which set sail at once. Because of the total darkness, they could observe little of Naha port and its environs.

The ship cast anchor outside Yamagawa harbor, in Satsuma, on the night of the twenty-ninth. The following day, before daybreak, the entire crew embarked on two boats and went ashore in the castle town of Kagoshima. The castaways, being strangers from another province, were taken in and out of the ship under cover of darkness, so that they couldn't see the shape of the harbor. As soon as they landed they were taken into custody at an assembly hall in Nishidamachi, and some of the clan's foot soldiers were detached to guard them in shifts. Satsuma was a mighty feudal demesne and its lord had issued a secret order to the guards to treat the castaways with the utmost courtesy. So the three captives were wined and dined daily on the rarest delicacies of land and sea, the choicest saké of the province. The lord sent them lavish gifts of summer kimono, underwear, and hemp robes, and even some winter *haori* and cotton-lined kimono, hardly needed in this midsummer month.

The castaways' interrogation dragged on day after day and the presiding official left no stone unturned in his questioning. One day, Lord Nariakira himself summoned them into his presence, and after offering them a lavish feast dismissed all his advisers and began to inquire in detail about the state of affairs in America. The three men had already shaved the crown of their heads in proper Japanese fashion and came to the audience dressed in the full ceremonial costumes they'd received. The lord had no interest in their outlandish foreign clothing anyway; what he wanted was all the information about political, educational, and military conditions in America he could get. He even asked about American customs and manners, such as wedding ceremonies and funeral rites. Denzō and Goemon's hearts shrank in the lord's presence, and they could hardly utter a coherent word. As always, it was John Man who summoned up his courage and told the lord how advanced American civilization was, giving him a number of concrete examples. The lord listened to his explanation, nodding slightly from time to time. But when John Man said that in America a man's value was judged by his ability, the lord gave an eager, vigorous nod.

The interrogation still went on, lasting forty-eight days in all. By its end, the following report from the lord of Satsuma to the Tokugawa government was compiled:

On the third day of the First Month of this year, three strange-looking men in a small rowing boat were stranded near the village of Mabunimagiri, in the Ryūkyūs. Officials of this clan who were sent to examine them found them to be: Denzō and his brother [actually his son] Goemon of Usaura, Takaoka district, in Tosa; and Manjirō of Nakanohama in the same province. The three above-mentioned men (as well as Denzō's younger brother Jūsuke and one Toraemon from the same village, Usaura) had embarked on a fishing excursion in the First Month, the Year of the Cow. However, they met with a severe storm and were driven to a desert island, lying in the direction of the Dragon. They survived chiefly on bird's meat until about the third day of the Sixth Month, when a foreign ship passed by and was beckoned to approach the island. Communicating in sign language, the men found that the ship was an American whaler. They asked for help and all five were taken aboard and delivered to a western province called Ōhō [sic!] in the Tenth Month of the same year. They were placed under the care of the captain's friends there, except for Manjirō, who agreed to be taken to the mainland. Setting sail in the Eleventh Month, the ship reached North America in the Fourth Month of the next year. After several years, Manjirō left there and crossed over to the province of Ōhō again, where they all earned their living, working mostly for a daily wage until they heard about an American ship bound for China. Their request to be conveyed to Japan on board this ship was refused, maritime traffic to Japan being closed as yet. They purchased their own boat and had it stowed aboard the ship, making arrangements to be put overboard as soon as Japanese shores were sighted. In the Tenth Month of last year, the three men left the foreign port (Jūsuke had died five years before of an ailment and Toraemon was left behind at his own request) and on the second day of the First Month, this year, they sighted the coast of the Ryūkyūs and had their boat put over the side. Wind and waves being too rough to allow a landing, they sought shelter behind a cliff and postponed their landfall until the next morning. Meanwhile, as they state, the ship had departed in a northwesterly direction. Had they been brought ashore by the foreign ship, we should have prevented their landing. But since they came ashore in a small craft, there was nothing that could be done about it. Their religious beliefs were carefully examined, but they claim to be innocent of any evil foreign heresy. Thus their accommodation in a common house became a possibility and they were taken care of locally until brought here for further questioning. This confirmed their above statements to be true in every respect. Such being the case, we have respectfully taken steps to deliver them under guard to the high commissioner of Nagasaki, where they should be arriving shortly.

All as above, in full respect, etc.

On this day, the eleventh of the Ninth Month.

Accordingly, the castaways were ordered to Nagasaki on the sixteenth of the Ninth Month. They left the castle town of Kagoshima by road and reached the port of Kyōdomari two days later. There they boarded a ship, and on the twenty-ninth arrived at Nagasaki. Their vessel was an eight-oared transport galley with thirteen sails, the bridle-crested flag of Satsuma flying on her mast and the clan's ensign hoisted in the bows.

On the first day of the Tenth Month they were taken ashore and sent to Lord Maki, the high commissioner, to be subjected to a further interrogation about their life abroad. Their statements were minutely recorded in a book called *The Reports of the Castaways*. The interrogation was completed in eighteen sessions, but their statements were no more than a repetition of what they had already said at Satsuma. They gave a detailed account of their careers from the day they left Tosa until their repatriation, the prevailing conditions of the various countries they'd visited, the manners and customs of their inhabitants, the food, industry, farm produce, geography, flora, wedding and funeral ceremonies, the political and military situation in these countries, etc., etc. One day they were asked whether thunderstorms existed in foreign countries, and did they also have four seasons? John Man's and his mates' observations weren't always correct; thus he says in *The Reports of the Castaways*, speaking of a telegraph:

A wire is stretched high above the road, and the written message attached to it, whence it travels from station to station by itself, unaided by a messenger. Outgoing messages are distinguished from incoming ones to avoid collision in midair; what kind of mechanism makes that possible is unknown to me. I presume that the letters are moved by the drawing power of magnetic steel. . . .

In a section called "Arithmetic" he makes this observation of a writing slate:

The principle of counting is the same abroad as in Japan. But their abacus is quite different from ours—it is a plate of thin purple stone, about one foot square with a wooden frame. They do their calculations with a tool that resembles a nail. When you wipe it with your fingers, the numerals all disappear.

This is how he describes a "steam carriage":

Carriages and horses are used for land transportation. Highways are built in a roundabout way to avoid going over mountains. They also have a steam car called a *rail-row* [sic] on which scores of people can travel without any effort on their part. They say that the mechanics of this vehicle are the same as a steamship's. I heard that this carriage had been prohibited recently, but didn't see one myself.

Yet compared to the observations of some previous castaways, John Man's comments were quite accurate on the whole. Speaking of the politics and economy of the Hawaiian Islands, he reports:

The capital is a place called Honolulu on Oahu, and it has become very prosperous in recent years. Ships from all parts of the world come to its port. The wealth of the seven Hawaiian Islands is estimated at about a hundred and twenty thousand silver coins, of which sixty thousand belong to the king of this territory, Kinikakeoli, and the other sixty thousand to the American governor, who owns about half the land. It is an excellent port of call, lying halfway along the Pacific sea voyage. If the Americans tried to take possession of these islands, England would surely protest. Though a small island country, it does not belong to either of them and its flag is a combination of the emblems of these three countries. All seven islands are rather mountainous, with some sandy flatland here and there;

rather than the five staple grains, it is more suited to growing potatoes and onions. They say that the hundred and twenty thousand silver coins of annual income are raised by taxes, mainly those levied from the international fleet of ships using the harbor.

He states the following about the American government:

The native people of America do not differ from Asians. Their complexion is rather dark. Since the country was founded originally by settlers from England, the major part of its population is still English. They tend to be a fair-skinned race, with a slightly yellow tinge to their eyes. They don't have a hereditary ruler, but elect their own "king" according to his knowledge and ability. After four years he is succeeded by another. When the rule of a king is good and his popularity with the masses lasting, he may sit on the throne for eight years. He lives a very simple life, rides on horseback when going out, and is accompanied by a single servant. There are some officials, but it is hard to tell them from ordinary civilians, since they don't flaunt their authority. The present king's name is Taylor. Five years ago, when there was a border dispute with Mexico which resulted in armed conflict, he led the attacking army to a great victory. This successful command brought him fame and glory, and ensured his election to king. He is an Englishman by blood. Yet though the country was founded by Englishmen, it does not belong to England. This year being the Year of the Rat, a new king is to succeed the present one.

About American criminal law he says:

The criminals are all free to move within a large enclosure and set to work at their own trades. The gravity of their crime determines the term of their imprisonment. Cloth and various other products are manufactured by the prisoners. A murderer is punished with the death penalty, performed as follows: a post is raised on a wooden scaffold. When the death sentence has been read out, a trapdoor below is released, the criminal falls through it, hanging by his neck, and he strangles to death. However, I have not seen an execution myself.

John Man had no knowledge of Commodore Perry's plan to visit Japan. The commodore's fleet arrived at Japanese shores two years later, in 1853, but John Man simply reports:

> Seven years ago, a warship from an American port called Boston embarked on a surveying cruise of various countries. Entering a Japanese port, I hear, she was ordered to leave at once and sailed away without accomplishing anything. When such surveying or whaling ships are blown off course by a storm, they run short of fresh water and fuel and must ask for permission to replenish their supply. Should permission be hard to obtain, they willingly leave a hostage. But to their amazement, the Japanese make a great fuss about such permits, as many detailed reports in American logbooks show. Generally speaking, the Japanese are quick-tempered, while the people over there are rather magnanimous. Besides, their country has an open-door policy at present, and definitely harbors no designs to invade and annex new territory. They have recorded and are aware of the fact that English ships have three times attempted to enter the Japanese port of Nagasaki, disguised as Dutch vessels, and three times their bluff was called and they were sent on their way empty-handed.... Sailing to China from California, a steamship carries so many passengers and such a load of their personal effects that it is impossible to haul a sufficient supply of coals for the entire voyage. The distance between America and China is 3,400 miles and no ship can make the long run to California without renewing her supply of fuel. It is my understanding that they wish to get some storage space for coal in Satsuma. I read as much in an American journal when I landed at Oahu last year.

At the end of the interrogation, on the twenty-first day of the Eleventh Month, they were put through the usual trial of stamping on Christ's image. John Man and Denzō were not Christian converts, but Goemon, while serving the Honolulu missionary, had often heard Christian sermons and prayed many a devout prayer, crossing himself and intoning "Amen, amen." Yet when he cheerfully stamped his feet on Christ's face he looked as innocent as a newborn babe. To please their interrogator, John Man and Denzō trampled long and hard on the image.

"How did you feel when you stamped on the image?" the official inquired.

"Rather cold," said Denzō, whose feet had become so accustomed to foreign footwear over the years that the bronze tablet chilled his bare soles.

When this last trial of *efumi* or "picture-stamping" was over, they were taken into custody at the house of detention in Sakura, an old castle town. To be thrown in jail again instead of being set free as he'd expected made John Man very angry and he got into a rebellious mood. Denzō, afraid that he might lose his temper, tried to soothe him in English, saying "Take it easy, boy, take it easy."

It was dark inside the jailhouse and some other prisoners were crouching in a corner of their cell. To avoid their eyes, John Man's party huddled together in another corner, when suddenly one of the men called: "Denzō-san, Manjirō-san!"

It was Torakichi and his four crew members of the *Tenju maru* from Hidaka in Kii, whom they had met in Honolulu. Torakichi told them how he and his men first reached China on the American ship, and then found passage on a Chinese junk bound for Nagasaki harbor. They were sentenced to three days in jail, as required by the law.

As the Kii men had said, the detention was no more than a formality and their treatment quite lenient. Lacking nothing, their only inconvenience was that they couldn't go out, somewhat like patients recuperating in quarantine after a long illness. When evening came, popular ballad-singers and puppeteers were invited to entertain them. A Jōruri singer sang the romance of *Osome Hisamatsu* at their request, and recited the story of *Shigure no kotatsu*, "The Hearth and the Rain." As he listened to the recital, John Man could savor again the soft, half-forgotten melody of the Japanese language. Denzō was so moved by the lyrics of the love-romance that he whispered, "I never realized how beautiful Japanese could be. . . ."

The three days passed and both the Kii and Tosa parties were released from prison.

The Tosa men were billeted in the house of Nishikawa Sanjirō, a government purveyor for their province. Their personal belongings which they had brought from America were restored to them, except for the things on the "forbidden import list": pistols, gunpowder, bullets, foreign books, their diaries in English, the nautical almanac, a sextant, gold dust, silver and copper coins. These articles were all confiscated by the government, as well as their boat, the *Adventure*, which had cost them a hundred dollars. That concluded the trial of the castaways. Now they had to wait at Nishikawa's house for an official from Tosa, who was coming to take them home. The Kōchi clan was already in receipt of the following notice, sent out a month earlier:

> We hereby notify you that Denzō and two other men from Usaura, Takaoka district, in the province of Tosa, who were rescued by a foreign whaling ship and later came ashore in the Ryūkyūs, were delivered to us by the lord of Satsuma. We request you to send some officials to the Nagasaki office where the above-mentioned will be released into your custody.

On receiving this notice, the Tosa clan appointed one of their vassals, a samurai by the name of Horibe Sasuke, to proceed as envoy to Nagasaki in the early part of the Sixth Month [1852]. Accompanied by some officials of junior rank, Horibe left Kōchi by sea and arrived in Nagasaki by the middle of that month. He then took John Man and his friends to the high commissioner's office, where they were issued letters of safe conduct:

> This is to certify that Denzō and his son Goemon of Usaura, Takaoka district, in the province of Tosa, the fief of Lord Matsudaira, as well as Nakahama Manjirō of Hata district in the same province, were stranded on a desert island in the Year of the Cow and later rescued by an American ship. Having lived in foreign countries for some years, they returned to the Ryūkyūs, and upon examination at this office as to their activities abroad, they were proved innocent of conversion to the Christian sect and other subversive influences; in short, they are fit to be returned to their native province. It is imperative, however, that they should hereafter not leave the said province and that we should be duly notified in the event of their deaths.
>
> Articles acquired or purchased abroad, such as gold dust, gold,

silver, copper or iron coins, guns, gunpowder, sextants, foreign dice, and the boat with its tackle, are to be confiscated. Japanese silver pieces will be granted in exchange for the gold dust and the foreign coins.

The above referred to and authorized by the Edo government; hence this notice.

The confiscated articles listed in the notice belonged for the most part to John Man. Denzō and Goemon had selected their possessions with careful regard for the government's prohibitions.

Escorted by envoy Horibe's party, the castaways left Nagasaki harbor on the twenty-fifth of the Sixth Month, a full year and a half after they had landed in the Ryūkyūs. On the thirtieth they sailed into the port of Urado and were ordered to lodge in one of Urado's inns. The next day, and on a succession of days afterward, they were summoned to the local office and interrogated once again. With a map of the world spread out before them, they had to give another account of the myriad things they had heard and seen in foreign lands. But John Man no longer had the name he was so proud of; to the officials, he was simply "Manjirō of Nakanohama." This interrogation was concluded on the twenty-fourth of the Ninth Month, and on the same day Manjirō went to see Denzō and Goemon safely to their old house in Usaura. But the house was gone without a trace, and so was Denzō's family. They had all died during his absence, and so father and son had to seek temporary accommodation in the house of some relatives. Manjirō arrived at his native village on the fifth of the Tenth Month, twelve years after he'd left home. He found his mother still alive and in good health.

KODANSHA AMERICA INC.

114 FIFTH AVENUE
NEW YORK, NEW YORK 10011

KODANSHA AMERICA INC.

Our aim is to promote cultural exchange between East and West.
We are interested in your suggestions.

Name of book purchased: _____

ISBN: _____

What subjects are you interested in?

☐ Home/Architecture (H) ☐ Papercraft (P) ☐ Needlecraft (N)
☐ Art (A) ☐ Literature (L) ☐ Social Sciences (S)
☐ Cooking (C) ☐ Floral Arts/Gardening (GN) ☐ Travel (T)
☐ Biography/Autobiography (BA) ☐ Health/Human Potential (HP) ☐ General (G)
☐ Business/Management (B) ☐ Language (LG) ☐ Encyclopedia (E)
☐ Craft (CR) ☐ Martial Arts/Sports (MA)

☐ Please send me your catalog.

NAME _____

STREET _____

CITY _____ STATE _____ ZIP _____

For Office Use only
• Request Code: PC
• Book Code:

Printed in Japan

8

Manjirō Boards a Government Ship and Sails to American Shores Once Again

In the following year, 1853, Commodore Perry's expedition made its surprise entrance into the port of Uraga. A great uproar shook the entire country, from the Tokugawa shogunate down to the last feudal clan in the provinces. Everyone was up in arms, and the slogan "Revere the Emperor and Expel the Barbarians" spread like wildfire throughout the realm. The Tokugawa government decided to invite Manjirō, the castaway from Tosa, to come to Edo, for he was well informed about America and fluent in its language. On the sixth day of the Eleventh Month, Manjirō was appointed superintendent in the office of the commissioner of public works with an annual income of twenty *koku* of rice and two retainers at his service. The obscure fisherman from Tosa, not allowed to live outside his province, awoke one morning a direct retainer of the shōgun. Thanks to the current of the times, he had won an unprecedented position in the government service of the day. Manjirō's nomination was mainly the idea of a senior cabinet minister, Lord Abe Masahiro, the governor of Ise. Lord Abe and his faction were aware of Manjirō's American training and set great store by him.

On the twenty-second of the Eleventh Month, Manjirō became an assistant to Egawa Tarōzaemon, the deputy governor in charge of navigation, surveying, and shipbuilding. Before appointing Manjirō to this new post, Lord Abe had his boat, the *Adventure*, brought to Edo for inspection and ordered several longboats built after this model. These became the predecessors of the Japanese longboat, later known as the *bateira* type. Lord Abe was a statesman of great wisdom and competence. As a young man of twenty-five, he had been promoted from high commissioner of shrines and temples to councillor to the shōgun, and at twenty-seven he became senior councillor. Not one among the shōgun's closest vassals could rival him in ability, reputation, or character. But Lord Ii Naosuke and Lord Tōdō Takayuki (governor of Izumi) of the rival party were busy intriguing to oust Lord Abe and he always carried a letter of resignation, dated the twenty-sixth of the Second Month, in his pocket when he attended the cabinet sessions. He supported the policy of opening the country for its long-term benefit to Japan, not for his own political influence or personal profit. The reason why he'd raised Deputy Governor Egawa to an important position was just another example of this. He wrote the following letter to the dockmaster, ordering the construction of a *bateira* longboat:

> As for the building of foreign-style boats, we would like you to model them exactly on the boat used by Nakahama Manjirō, a subject of Governor Matsudaira of Tosa, to land on our shores, the same boat that was sent to us from Nagasaki.

Lord Abe, aiming at the modernization of the shōgun's navy, had realized the importance of surveying home waters and studying the modern science of navigation. But to build and equip a fleet of large ships according to foreign models was beyond the power of the bankrupt Tokugawa economy; what was worse, they had even failed to train their sailors in modern navigation and Lord Abe had to ask Manjirō to come up with a contingency plan. But he was soon to be replaced in the Senior Council—as the shōgun's cabinet was called—by Hotta Masayoshi, and two years later, in the prime of his life, he passed away at the age of thirty-nine.

Manjirō proposed a government-controlled whaling business to the shogunate. It would not only bring in a profit from whaling operations, but would offer the crews training opportunities in surveying and navigation, thus killing the proverbial two birds with one stone. The government adopted this proposal in 1859.

In the Second Month of that year, Manjirō was put in charge of the proposed whaling business as its general manager. Working closely with Mochizuki Taishō and Kai Naojirō, who had both been trained in gunnery by Egawa Tarōzaemon, he refitted a government warship into a whaling schooner. The vessel, which had been built solely by Japanese shipwrights, was equipped with whaleboats and other necessary gear and named the *No. 1*, in the Kimizawa class.

When Admiral Putyatin came to Shimoda on board the *Diana*, a Russian man-of-war, to conclude treaties with Japan, his ship was damaged by a major earthquake. As they were towing her away to Heta for repairs, she was hit by a storm and capsized. To replace the sunken vessel, several hundred Japanese carpenters were hired to build one according to the designs of the *Diana*'s Russian engineer. It took them three months to complete the construction. The master shipwright who was in charge of this task was later ordered by the government to build six ships of the same Kimizawa class; the name was taken from a local district.

Manjirō sailed the *No. 1* as far as the Bonins in search of whales, but before he could find any the ship ran into a terrible storm. On the verge of foundering, they had to cut down one of her masts and barely managed to find refuge in Shimoda harbor on the Izu Peninsula. When the wind abated, they sailed back to Shinagawa Bay. Manjirō started planning another whaling expedition right away, but the Tokugawa government had its hands full just then with the question of sending a delegation to America for the ratification of a treaty between the two nations. The choice of Manjirō, so well versed in America's life-style and language, as official interpreter for the foreign mission was to be expected.

The delegation, a party of seventy-seven, headed by the chief envoy, Lord Shinmi of Buzen, and his deputy, Lord Muragaki of Awaji, left Shinagawa on board the U.S. warship *Powhatan* in the Second Month of 1860. It was followed by the Japanese warship *Kanrin maru* with the shipping commissioner, Lord Kimura of Settsu, Captain Katsu Rintarō, Fukuzawa Yukichi, and Nakahama Manjirō, altogether about ninety men on board. The *Kanrin maru* was a warship bought from the Dutch by the Tokugawa government and equipped with a steam engine of about a hundred horsepower. Coal was used only when entering or leaving port; once in the open sea she worked like any other sailing ship—a convenient combination of the new and the old.

The *Powhatan* touched at Honolulu on her way, while the *Kanrin maru* sailed directly to San Francisco, arriving in its harbor on March 17 according to the Western calendar. In a book called *The Secret His-*

tory of California's Civilization, Kawamura quotes some contemporary American newspaper articles. San Francisco's *Alta California* reported the event on March 18, 1860, in a full-page editorial headlined "Arrival of Japanese Steamship":

> A warship of the Japanese Imperial Navy, the *Kanrin maru*, made port at San Francisco yesterday afternoon, casting anchor by the wharf on Vallejo Street. Commanded by Captain Katsu Rintarō, she took thirty-seven days to complete the journey from Uraga in Japan. Lord Kimura of Settsu, an admiral in the Japanese navy, is among the passengers on board the ship. The objective of this warship's visit here is to act as a sort of harbinger for the U.S.S. *Powhatan* which left Edo on February 10 and is now en route to this country, carrying a delegation of Japanese envoys....
>
> The *Kanrin maru*'s voyage went smoothly and was a pleasant one without any untoward incidents. The visiting officials all seem very polite and well behaved....
>
> Four retainers follow the admiral wherever he goes, always ready to wait upon him with great deference. But he seems to be a man of considerable wisdom, who would never treat his vassals as slaves. Some of the crew, wearing black overcoats, pants, and Japanese-style straw sandals, cast bewildered glances at us from the deck. Each man has a large square badge on his back, with his rank written on it in Japanese letters.
>
> These sailors look far better educated than our California Chinamen. They keep a clean ship, with every item neatly stowed in its place according to regulations. We had the pleasure of being taken on a complimentary tour of the ship and meeting Admiral Kimura in his cabin. He is an affable, kindly-looking gentleman of forty, apparently not lacking in goodwill; all in all, we felt, a man formidably suited for his important mission. When we entered his room, Lord Kimura was just having his hair made up into a most stylish coiffure by one of his retainers. Squatting on the floor, His Lordship seemed to be thoroughly enjoying the shampooing of his scalp. But when he emerged on deck only minutes later, he was in full ceremonial costume with snow-white socks on his feet, a dark-

brown overcoat, and a magnificent skirt of indigo blue, tied in front with a silver cord. At his side, the admiral wore a set of long and short swords, displayed by all Japanese officials; their blades are beautifully polished and extremely sharp. . . . It is reported that Captain Katsu had been indisposed for most of the voyage, bedridden by sea-sickness.

All the articles written by contemporary American journalists about their impressions of the Japanese show an extraordinary amount of good-will. *The Secret History of California's Civilization* has excerpts from every variety of newspaper, but virtually all of them give the Japanese visitors a kind welcome. The editorials also show a great deal of curiosity about the strange customs of the Japanese; here are several examples:

Lord Kimura of Settsu and his party landed at San Francisco, their first visit to our shores, and were escorted to the International Hotel. In the lobby they met formally with the mayor of San Francisco and other dignitaries of the city. It was a rare sight to see all the Japanese officials squatting on the carpet covering the floor except Lord Kimura, who sat on a sofa, when Governor Downey of California appeared to greet the esteemed guests. The Japanese party thought it very strange that someone purporting to be the governor of a state should appear in public without a solemn procession of his retainers. Not followed by a single servant?—this man must surely be an impostor, they all thought. Captain Brooke did his best to assuage their doubts, explaining over and over again that this was indeed the real governor of California. But the Japanese officials still kept glancing at the doorway and inspecting Governor Downey from head to foot, shaking their heads in disbelief and obviously thinking: a man without a ceremonial retinue at his heels can't be the true governor. Yet at long last the lord of Settsu did exchange formal greetings with the governor through his interpreter, Mr. Manjirō, and both gentlemen expressed their views on the exciting events of that day. . . . In his address, the governor said how pleased he was to welcome Lord Kimura and his party on American soil, calling them harbingers of a new friendship between the two nations separated by the Pacific, which are now opening trade relations....

After the official banquet, Lord Kimura's delegation was accompanied back to their ship by the city's dignitaries and officers of the U.S. navy. That evening, San Franciscans watched in fascination as a stately train of Japanese samurai came to meet them on the wharf, waving paper lanterns on long poles to the throbbing rhythm of large drums....

Alta California

Lord Kimura of Settsu and Captain Katsu exchanged handshakes with everyone present, bowing politely in Japanese style, while Nakahama Manjirō acted as interpreter. After he announced the full name and rank of every person to be introduced, Lord Kimura received him in a gentlemanly and refined way. This spectacle lasted about twenty minutes, during which the room became more and more crowded as new curious bystanders arrived. Everybody was doing his best to be friends, since the event was considered to be of great consequence to America as well, creating the vehicle to develop trade and other relations between the two nations. On that day, the Japanese came out dressed splendidly in their full regalia, each man with the set of long and short swords at his side. Lord Kimura's ceremonial robe was particularly beautiful. Their costume is completely different from what the Chinese wear....

A banquet was held in the great hall of the hotel in honor of the Japanese guests.... They tasted only a small portion of every course, but seemed satisfied with the food. Captain Katsu, when served ice cream, called it "snow" or "ice." "What do you call it in your country?" someone asked him. *"Berri gutto,"* answered the captain.

Alta California, March 23

The captain of the Japanese warship, Katsu Rintarō, speaks English as if reading a textbook. He is never seen with a hat on. The pate of his head is always clean-shaven, and his hair tends to stand up in bristles, but it is tied into a knot that points forward. All the Japanese officials wear a similar hairdo. About half a dozen of the highest-ranking men wear wide-brimmed hats, resembling the umbrellas favored by our California Chinese on rainy days. The rest of them wear straw bonnets, tied firmly under their chins with a cord lest they should be blown away. The sailors wear nothing on their heads, and some have their pates smoothly shaven in the style of old bonzes.... The officials are all well dressed, but instead of shoes they wear hemp-soled sandals, made of grass.

Sacramento Union, March 23

A week later, on March 29, the *Powhatan* with the rest of the Japanese delegation on board reached San Francisco.

Newspapermen were allowed to visit the ship as soon as she made port. The Japanese delegation had occupied all the cabins on both sides of the quarterdeck. We understand that throughout the long voyage there wasn't a single quarrel among the party. There are two or three other interpreters present among the delegation, but none of them can compare with Mr. Manjirō of the *Kanrin maru*. Most likely, it will be interpreter Manjirō who will accompany the delegates to the federal capital of Washington, although many of the Japanese attendants have picked up a fair amount of English during the passage. Only a small part of the group fell prey to seasickness, the majority of the delegation being in fine spirits throughout the journey. Rice was served with their meals, prepared by a specially appointed Japanese chef.

Alta California, March 30

After the magnificent reception at San Francisco, the delegation boarded the U.S.S. *Powhatan* again and headed for Panama. Crossing the isthmus by train, they boarded the *Roanoke*, an American man-of-war, on the Atlantic side and soon reached Washington, D.C. The American government gave them a welcome reserved for national guests, placing as many as sixty rooms in one of Washington's best hotels, Willard's, at the party's disposal. Since the founding of the United States, the capital had not seen its administration, the army, and the navy give a warmer welcome to any foreign delegation.

The envoys, Lord Shinmi of Buzen and Lord Muragaki of Awaji, were received in audience by President Buchanan and exchanged the notes of ratification of the Japanese–American treaty. On May 13, they were given a gala send-off by the American public and officialdom, and embarked on the *Niagara* (4580 tons), one of America's new giant ships. Sailing around the Cape of Good Hope, they touched at Java and Hong Kong and arrived at Shinagawa on November 9.

Unfortunately the *Kanrin maru* had suffered some damage on the trip out, which had to be repaired at once. The repairs completed, she could only leave San Francisco on her homeward journey, and Manjirō was unable to join the Washington delegation.

He had bought many "articles of civilization" in San Francisco, such as a sewing machine and a photographic apparatus. But when the pictures taken with this machine were developed, they showed a man's kimono folded on the left side. Before taking a picture, one had to fold the kimono on the wrong left side, and wear one's swords on the equally wrong right side. He also went out with Fukuzawa Yukichi, and each bought a Webster's dictionary—without doubt the first two English dictionaries that were ever openly imported to Japan.

During his stay in San Francisco, Manjirō often visited the city's public offices in his function of interpreter, wondering at how much the city had changed in a mere decade. The place he'd known had been a picture of chaos, a disorderly heap of goods, boxes and barrels streaming in from all over the world, its streets rivers of stinking mud whenever it rained. He remembered a notice board on one of the street corners which said, "Not even an idiot could walk down this street." A filthy town full of violent men who took the law into their own hands and others who trampled on them had changed into a new city with many blocks of tall buildings and wide avenues where elegant ladies and gentlemen promenaded.

On her way home the *Kanrin maru* put in at Honolulu, and the Japanese party was received in audience by the tribal king of the islands, Kamehameha. Manjirō went to see Toraemon the cooper and other old acquaintances and friends. It had been eleven years since he last saw them, and they had many a story to share. All his old friends looked in wonder at the two swords by his side, saying happily: "Well, John Man is certainly getting on in the world."

9

Manjirō Becomes Adviser to a Mighty
Clan in Times of Trouble

The *Kanrin maru* entered the port of Uraga on June 23, 1860.

Manjirō's valuable contribution as interpreter throughout the voyage was recognized by both his superiors and the ship's crew and he was awarded thirty pieces of silver. But becoming a government official wasn't the height of his ambition; what he really wanted was to outfit a good whaling ship and take her out on a whale hunt in the far, wide oceans. He kept proposing whaling operations to the feudal government, until they relieved him of his current post of naval instructor on October 9, 1860. Two years later, he was appointed captain of his old *No. 1* again. At last, his long-cherished dream to be a whaling skipper was coming true.

The *No. 1* was loaded with shipbuilding material and parts, and Manjirō, the crew, and two midshipmen (instructors of navigation)—Hayashinami Gonnojo and Hayashi Waichirō—sailed out of Shinagawa in January 1863. Reaching the Bonins in February, they started building whaleboats, using the material brought from Shinagawa. In about two months, the boats were ready to go, and on May 4 Manjirō and his crew set out on a whale hunt. By early June they had caught two sperm whales—not a bad result for their maiden cruise.

Among the foreign sailors Manjirō had hired in the Bonins was a vicious bully, a man who'd roar and curse all day, picking fights at the slightest provocation. When someone tried to restrain him, he'd pull an ugly-looking knife and go for the man's throat. He was completely lawless, most likely a pirate who had fallen on bad days. With such a sinister character on board, it was hard to maintain discipline. It would have been easy enough to get rid of him with one fast stroke of the sword, but Manjirō was afraid it might be viewed as the lynching of a foreigner and cause a good deal of trouble. For the same reason, it was risky to simply dump him on a desert island; Manjirō had to leave the Bonins on June 16 and sail all the way back to Uraga in order to hand this ruffian over to the authorities.

Manjirō unloaded his barrels of whale oil and started to prepare for another whaling expedition. But he wasn't allowed to sail, for the feudal government found itself in a most painful deadlock: back in the summer of 1859 when they were negotiating border questions with the Russians in Edo, some "anti-barbarian" *rōnin* attacked and killed a Russian officer and a prolonged national crisis followed.

Muraviev-Amurski, the governor of Siberia, had successfully concluded the Aihun treaty with China which recognized the Amur region as Russian territory. Encouraged by this diplomatic breakthrough, the Russian governor and his fleet made a triumphant entry into Edo Bay in the summer of 1859. Russian advances in the Balkans had been hindered by France and England during the Crimean War, but now Russia was taking advantage of the hostility flaring up between France and England to pursue a historic policy of working its way deeper and deeper into Asia.

China, badly weakened by the Taiping Rebellion of Hung Hsiu-Ch'üan, yielded to Governor Muraviev's demands without protest. Japan too was going through a critical period in its internal affairs, caused by the rioting of "anti-barbarian" zealots. Many feared that the island of Sakhalin might have to be relinquished. Governor Muraviev sailed his fleet of seven warships into the waters off Shinagawa and opened negotiations on the border question of Sakhalin and Russian fishery rights aboard his flagship. The talks were continued at Tentoku Temple in Shiba, and Russian officers of the fleet came ashore five times, visiting the city of Edo on horseback or on foot. They went sightseeing to Shinagawa, the Zōjō Temple, Atagoyama, Nihonbashi, Asakusa, and the Inari Shrine at Ōji. Of course they were mocked, abused, even stoned by the Edo populace wherever they went. But Russian military men were used to this sort of welcome from other parts of the world, mainly the regions along the Black Sea, and weren't overly concerned as they strolled through the city on their shore leave.

Then in the evening of August 25 an Ensign Mofet of the Russian navy took two bluejackets ashore in Yokohama to get some provisions

134

in one of the harbor stores. As they were leaving the shop, a gang of Japanese suddenly attacked them with naked blades. The first sword blow caught Mofet on the nape of the neck, and two stabs into his shoulder and back followed as he went down. One of the sailors was cut down with a single sword stroke, the other took a wound in his left arm and sought refuge in the shop. The shopkeeper brought his shutters down at once, locking out the assassins. When the Russians came running to the spot, the killers had already made their getaway. Ensign Mofet was rushed to a hospital in the American settlement and given first-aid treatment, but succumbed to his wounds after four hours of agony.

This incident further complicated the troubled border dispute; both parties got more stubborn and the talks ended in deadlock. Governor Muraviev and his fleet weighed anchor from Edo Bay, leaving behind one warship to enforce some kind of settlement in his officer's assassination case. His attempt to annex Sakhalin had failed during this round of negotiations, but to prepare leverage for future claims, the governor had large numbers of Russian convicts shipped to the island. The Japanese government was already sending a delegation to Europe to seek a postponement in the opening of Japanese ports. In 1861, realizing the need for dealing with this grave situation, it ordered its envoys to negotiate a settlement of the Sakhalin border dispute. Arriving in the Russian capital, they conferred with the deputy minister of foreign affairs from August 21 to September 12 of 1862 and reached an understanding that both parties would send a commission to survey the actual situation on the island and then arrive at a final agreement. The Russians sent their commission to Sakhalin in August 1863, demanding that the Japanese do likewise, but the Tokugawa government was so preoccupied with the Chōshū War, and with putting down rebellion, that it failed to send any of its own representatives. The Russian delegation accused the Japanese government of reneging on its contract and left the island.

The national crisis had gone from bad to worse with the Tsushima Incident in March 1861. British warships had been active in the Korean Straits for some time, and in January one of their cruisers began surveying the Tsushima coast. When the Russians learned about this, they notified the shogunate that the English obviously harbored aggressive designs and that the czar's government was ready to offer military help in defense of Tsushima. Although the Japanese side declined their offer, a Russian battleship, the *Posadnik*, suddenly arrived at Tsushima on March 13 and landed a navy unit under the pretext of making repairs to the ship. They laid claim to a stretch of territory, cut down trees without permission, and surveyed the coast. In April they built a colony of typical Russian cottages in the harbor, and in May murdered a Tsushima clansman who was in charge of the local observation post; in short, they behaved in an utterly reckless and arrogant manner.

The incident was quickly reported by the Tsushima authorities to the high commissioner of Nagasaki and the Tokugawa government, and Lord Oguri of Bungo, the commissioner for foreign countries, was dispatched to Tsushima to demand the withdrawal of the Russians. But they refused to leave the island; on the contrary, in June another Russian warship arrived and the two captains led a landing force of about forty bluejackets ashore, and insisted on a meeting with the feudal lord of the demesne. They demanded the right to defend the port and to occupy the area between Imozaki and Hirugaura. The shōgun's officials, at their wits' end, asked the British minister to Japan to act as mediator and also pleaded with the Russian consul at Hakozaki to use his influence to make the Russian warships leave Tsushima. It was, however, mainly the British intervention that forced the two warships to withdraw in the end.

The authority of the shōgun's government was completely undermined, the flames of rebellion against the Tokugawas burning higher and brighter than ever. The final test that revealed the impotence of their government to the whole nation was the Chōshū War. The high and mighty rulers of yesteryear had lost all will to devise a constructive policy, and the course of events pointed to one inevitable outcome: their supremacy must collapse. To fit out a whaling schooner in wild times like these was obviously out of the question, and Manjirō resigned himself to the situation. Reining in his urge to make new proposals for whaling operations, the skipper of Japan's No. 1 waited for the next opportunity with folded arms. Not that he was idling away his time—he was busy as ever, for when Yokohama was declared an open port, all kinds of people who felt the need to learn English, or have their mistakes corrected, came rushing to him. Even daimyō, some lesser lords, and an official retainer or two came to see him frequently, some of them asking inane questions like "What's the name of this or that bird, animal, or plant?" It was often more than Manjirō could stand.

When he had time to spare, he translated the *Table of Logarithms* into Japanese and put a special effort into teaching English to a class of volunteers. These were men of as different a social background and age as one could imagine, coming from scholarly circles, the shōgun's group of direct retainers, and some from the ragged *rōnin* legion. Where they had learned their bit of English was hard to tell, but one thing was certain: their pronunciation was far from standard American. They would pronounce "United States" as *Anatessu Sutatesu*, and the word "because" became *bekayūzu* in their strange diction. There was even someone who pronounced "reason" as *rē-asson*. Manjirō did his best to bring these odd sounds closer to the language he'd heard in America; among his students there were brilliant men who were later to play their roles in the making of modern Japan, such as Hosokawa Junjirō, Mitsukuri Rinshō, Ōtori Keisuke, and others.

In the first year of Genji [1864], on November 11, the shogunate loaned the *No. 1* to the Satsuma clan for three months at the request of its feudal lord. The clan planned to use her as a training boat for teaching warship navigation to their cadets. The lord had issued an invitation to the ship's captain as well and Manjirō went down to Kagoshima, where he taught English and the art of navigation to a group of eager young samurai. He had an old bond of sorts with Satsuma; it was this southern clan, after all, that had interrogated them when they came back from their wanderings. But when the clan rose against the Tokugawa government together with some other demesnes, Manjirō resigned from his post and returned to Edo in January 1868.

Later that year, Manjirō was employed by the Kōchi clan and given a fief worth a hundred *koku* of rice a year. He was appointed instructor of English at the Kaisei School and given the scholarly rank of "Doctor-Preceptor of the Sixth Grade." But next year he had to retire from this post for reasons of health and recuperated at one of the official estates of the Tosa clan in the Honjō Ward of Edo. In August 1879, he was ordered to travel to Europe with Ōyama Iwao and his military mission to observe the action in the Franco-Prussian War, but he never reached the battlefield, for an illness forced him to stay in London. On the way back, he made a brief stop in America, paying a visit to the Whitfields at Fairhaven, where his benefactor was still alive. Fondly recalling the grand old days, the two seamen couldn't hold back their tears. Manjirō didn't forget to call on his many old friends in Hawaii as well.

In the fifth year of Meiji [1872] he relapsed into ill health and resigned himself to the quiet life of an aging recluse. But one memory still brought a youthful thrill to his heart: a well-rigged schooner on a whale hunt, sailing the deep, wide seas. Manjirō's eternal dream. . . .

He died on November 12, 1898, at the age of seventy-one and is buried in the graveyard of the Temple of the Holy Heart at Yanaka, in Tokyo.

Notes on "A Geisha Remembers"

Page 17 **Fukagawa**
A district in the western part of Kōtō Ward in modern Tōkyō. One of the *un*licensed pleasure quarters of Edo, with particular appeal for devotees of the arts. Geisha from here distinguished themselves by wearing the *haori* overcoat when it was still male attire, and some refused to sell their sexual favors for money. Fukagawa was shut down during the reforms mentioned in the story.

Takashima Shūhan
Born in Nagasaki, Takashima (1798–1866) began to study military science quite early in his life, but first came to prominence in about 1840 when, acting on what he had learned about the Opium War between Britain and China, he recommended the adoption of Western-style ordnance to the Bakufu. After exciting the jealousy of his superiors, he was imprisoned for some years, but was reinstated after Commodore Perry's arrival in 1853. Virtually all the artillery specialists of the period were his pupils. "Shūhan" is his Buddhist name, given posthumously.

a mild form of exile
That is, exclusion from strategic ports and cities such as Edo, Ōsaka, and Nagasaki, as well as the major national highways.

Kiyomoto style of ballad
A form of the Jōruri ballad characterized by a soft and gentle rhythm, which was developed in the mid-Edo period and named after its author Kiyomoto. It was often used as an accompaniment to dance or drama.

Hongoku
The present location of this district is in the northwest corner of Chūō Ward in central Tōkyō.

Temple of the Goddess of Mercy
A famous temple in the Asakusa area dedicated to the goddess Kannon (from the Chinese Kuan-yin, who was originally a male deity).

Descended from the Indian bodhisattva Avalokiteśvara, Kannon became a goddess of love, somewhat comparable to the Virgin Mary in the West. Her temple was the site of a yearly festival.

Page 18 **unicorn ivory**
"Unicorn" is from the original Japanese, but refers to the tusk growing from the skull of a narwhal, sometimes found on beaches. The unicorn legend supposedly arose from its resemblance to the skull of a horse.

Page 19 **Senjugawara**
Commonly known as Senju, this district lies in the Adachi Ward of Tōkyō. At one time it was a prosperous post station on the Nikkō Highway.

Great Halberd Festival
This is *tamaboko no omatsuri* in the original but is more often called *okunchi*. It originated with the harvest festival at the Suwa Shrine, and continues over three days in early October. There is a parade of portable shrines, a dragon dance, and a procession with decorative halberds resembling parasols.

Matsumoto Kōshirō
A famous Kabuki actor (1764–1838) of the period. He was the son of Matsumoto Kōshirō IV, and succeeded to the name in 1801.

Page 20 **Lord Egawa Tarōzaemon**
Born in Nirayama on the Izu Peninsula, Egawa (1801–55) was a student of Dutch surveying and military science under Takashima Shūhan. Active in the movement for civilian government and the improvement of coastal defense, he became an important Bakufu official. He founded a school to teach Takashima's theories and built Japan's first reverberatory furnace, which made it possible to cast proper cannon at home instead of importing them. Egawa's collected writings quote discussions with Takashima and may have been the inspiration for Ibuse's story.

Ōshio Heihachirō
A Confucian scholar (1793–1837) who served as a constable in the city of Ōsaka and later became well known as a public inspector. Adopting the unorthodox philosophy of Wang Yang-ming (called Yōmeigaku in Japanese), which proposes the unity of knowledge and action, he sold his books and used the money to feed the poor. He became their spiritual adviser and, during the famine of 1837, led them in an ill-fated rebellion. Rice merchants' warehouses were broken into and the food distributed, but after a single day the uprising was crushed and

Ōshio went into hiding. When he was found after forty days or so, he committed suicide. His story is told in Ivan Morris's *The Nobility of Failure*. It is interesting that the same Wang Yang-ming philosophy motivated Mishima Yukio's abortive coup.

Torii Yōzō

Offspring of the official Confucian scholar Hayashi Jussai, Torii Yōzō (1804–74) was adopted by the learned Torii family. In 1837, he became a *metsuke* (superintendent, but sometimes translated as "spy") and started persecuting scholars of Western science. In 1841, he was appointed town magistrate (*machibugyō*) of Edo, an office that combined administrative, judicial, and police powers. He became commissioner of accounts in 1843, and attempted to serve Senior Councillor Mizuno Tadakuni by introducing the Tempō Reforms (as they were known) to put the economy back on a firmer footing. In 1844, after these measures, which combined harsh sumptuary laws with harassment of progressive scholars, had failed, he was demoted and banished to the remote province of Sanuki.

druifkogel

Dutch for "grapeshot."

Sakuma Shōzan

Originally from Shinano, Sakuma Shōzan (1811–64) was sent by his feudal lord to Edo, where his studies ranged from neo-Confucianism to Western gunnery. He was impressed by Takashima Shūhan's artillery demonstration of 1841, and became a pupil of Egawa Tarōzaemon. Xenophobic at first, he came round to the view that Japan should be opened to the outside world. He formed his own group of scholars and one of them, Yoshida Shōin, tried to leave the country illegally on one of Commodore Perry's ships (as Robert Louis Stevenson relates in his essay on Yoshida). Arrested for complicity, Sakuma was not released until 1862. Two years later, he was assassinated by anti-foreign fanatics.

Kawaji Saemon

Beginning his career as inspector of the Treasury, Kawaji Saemon (1801–68) later served as city commissioner of Nara and Ōsaka. In 1852, he was appointed commissioner of the Treasury and chief of coastal defense. In 1853, he led official negotiations with the Russian envoy in Nagasaki. He became commissioner for foreign countries in 1863, but shot himself the day after foreigners were allowed into Edo.

Honda of Etchū

Honda Tadanori, who succeeded his father as lord of Izumi Castle in Mutsu in 1836. In 1843 he became a junior councillor. Mainly in charge of foreign affairs, he was still active in 1860.

Ōtsuki Bankei
A Confucian scholar (1801–78) and tutor of the Sendai fief. A student of Western gunnery, he advocated the opening of Japanese ports to foreign shipping.

the plain of Tokumaru
Now part of Itabashi Ward in Tōkyō.

Senior Councillor Mizuno
Mizuno Tadakuni (1794–1851), lord of the sixty-thousand-*koku* domain of Hamamatsu, to which he moved in 1817. Besides being governor of Echizen, he held various official posts such as commissioner of shrines and temples before being appointed senior councillor (*rōjū*) in 1834. After the death of Shōgun Tokugawa Ienari, he instituted the Tempō Reforms in 1841. After their failure he was demoted. He was briefly reinstated, but he was held responsible for the injustices of Torii Yōzō (see note for page 20), who rose to power while he was in office. His domain was reduced, he was retired and put under house arrest, and he finally died in despair.

Page 23 ### Inoue Sadayū
Full name, Inoue Sadayū Masamichi. His ancestor, Inoue Masatsugu, distinguished himself at the siege of Ōsaka Castle in 1615, and his post of artillery officer to the shōgun had descended through generations to Sadayū, who was dismissed in the thirteenth year of the Tempō era (1842).

Tatsuke Shirōbei
Full name, Tatsuke Shirōbei Naokiyo. Another hereditary artilleryman, who was rewarded for ordering a special gun for Prince Iesada in 1825. He resigned in 1842 for reasons of "health."

Page 24 ### Takano Chōei
A physician (1804–50) from northern Honshū who made a study of Dutch internal medicine. He went to Nagasaki in 1822 to become a pupil of Siebold, the German scientist who gave (and got) a great deal of information in his dealings with Japanese scholars before being expelled in 1830. Takano eventually opened a practice in Edo and was one of the founding members of Watanabe Kazan's study group, the notorious Shōshikai (Old Men's Club). In 1838, he published a critique of Bakufu policies called *Yume monogatari* (The Tale of a Dream) and was imprisoned for it the following year. He escaped in 1845 during a fire and lived for some years under the name Sawa Sampaku. After years of wandering, translating, and teaching friendly daimyō who

were interested in military science, he was finally traced by Bakufu agents in 1850 and committed suicide after killing one of them.

Watanabe Kazan
A painter (1793–1841) of the southern (*nanga*) school from Mikawa (presently Aichi Prefecture). In 1832, he was transferred to Edo as an adviser to the government on coastal defense. A man of wide-ranging interests, he founded the Old Men's Club for liberal-minded intellectuals such as Takano Chōei (see note above) and Ozeki Sanei (see note for page 30) to study Western science and world affairs. In 1839 he published his *shinkiron*, confronting the government on its outmoded defense policy. For this he was at first sentenced to death (there is a self-portrait of him standing between the two officials who delivered the sentence). Through the efforts of his many friends and followers, he was released to spend the rest of his life under house arrest. However, people of his own clan who were envious of his influence spread a rumor that further charges were in store. Already broken in health, and concerned that his liege lord would be further discredited, Watanabe put an end to his life in 1841.

the famous mathematician Dr. Uchida
Uchida Itsumi (1805–?), also known under the *nom de plume* of Kansai. A mathematician of the Seki school, he also studied astronomy and later contributed to the reform of the calendar.

Page 27 **Honjō Moheiji**
A real person, said to have been in Takashima Shūhan's service at one time. He went over to Takashima's rival, Fukuda Kurōbei, and eventually helped Torii Yōzō to entrap his former master.

Page 30 **Kanazawa**
Refers to the present Yokohama Bay, not to the Kanazawa on the Sea of Japan.

Shiba
In this period, a residential district for samurai, with many shrines and temples. Now part of Minato Ward, facing Tōkyō Bay.

Suzuki Shunzan
Another scholar of Dutch medicine and Western gunnery (1801–46). Like Watanabe Kazan, he came from the Tawara domain in Mikawa. He studied European military science under Takano Chōei (see note for page 24).

Ozeki Sanei
A scholar and physician (1787–1839) from Tsuruoka in the northern

province of Dewa (now Akita and Yamagata prefectures). In Edo, he studied Dutch learning and later became a pupil of Siebold in Nagasaki. He served the shogunate as an astronomer and translator. A member of Watanabe Kazan's Old Men's Club, he committed suicide when it was broken up.

Tsubaki Chinzan
A painter of the southern school from Edo (1801–54). He first studied painting under one of Watanabe Kazan's students, later under Kazan himself. He is known chiefly for his portraits and bird-and-flower (*kachō*) sketches. When his master was thrown in jail, Tsubaki was active in the movement to free him, and in the meantime took care of Kazan's family. His most famous work is a portrait of Kazan.

Itō Gemboku
A physician from Hizen (now Nagasaki Prefecture) in Kyūshū (1800–71). After studying Western medicine with Siebold, he moved to Edo and opened his own practice. He published a twenty-four-volume work on medicine and in 1831 became official physician to the Hizen fief. In 1846 he succeeded in developing a cowpox vaccine, and was appointed head of the innoculation center at Kanda in Edo in 1858. Afterward, he became official physician to the Bakufu.

Togawa
Togawa Yasukiyo became a justice of the Nagasaki magistracy in 1835. He left the office in 1842 and took up the post of chief treasurer in the following year. In 1866, he applied for retirement on account of advanced age.

Taguchi
Taguchi Yoshiyuki became a justice of the Nagasaki magistracy in 1839, but retired from the office in 1841.

Chief Interpreter Kōjiro
The Kōjiro family served the Nagasaki magistracy for generations as official interpreters. This reference is most likely to Kōjiro Tokujirō, who became chief interpreter in 1841.

Master Ikebe of the house of Hosokawa
Ikebe Keita (1798–1868) was a pioneer in the use of Western artillery in the Kumamoto clan of Kyūshū. He had begun by studying surveying, then decided to apply his knowledge practically by learning from the artillery expert Takashima Shirōbei and his son Shūhan.

Page 31 ### Izawa, governor of Mimasaka
Izawa Masayoshi succeeded Togawa (see note for page 30) as justice

146

in 1842, and left the magistracy in 1845. In 1861, he held the post of chief superintendent (*ōmetsuke*).

Lord Tokugawa of Mito
That is, Tokugawa Nariaki (1800–60), the head of the Mito clan. A patron of learning and the arts, he established a clan school in 1841. He directed the clan's policy toward reform of the military system, and encouraged the casting of new guns. Although he was related to the ruling dynasty, the Bakufu resented his efforts and in 1844 he was placed under house arrest. Later he was pardoned and in 1853, when Commodore Perry arrived in Japan, he participated in the Bakufu's policy-making. But after clashing with a senior minister over the successor to Shōgun Iesada, he retired into seclusion for the remainder of his life.

Page 33   ***chobokure* ballad**
Also called *chongare*. These were satirical songs, especially popular in the pleasure quarters. Originally satires on general social problems, they became increasingly political as the era of Bakufu rule drew on.

Page 36   **the scholarly family Hayashi**
Hayashi Razan (1583–1657) was the distinguished ancestor of this family. He was the chief exponent of the neo-Confucianist philosophy of Chu Hsi to the early shogunate, and his descendants became hereditary "state philosophers."

Page 39   **Kodemma**
A district in the northern part of Chūō Ward in Tōkyō.

Page 40   **Fukuda Kurōbei**
Fukuda was Takashima Shūhan's superior until the latter was promoted (see note for page 17).

Page 42   **Ezo**
The old name for Hokkaidō, which was settled only recently. The "string of islands" includes Sakhalin (Japanese: Karafuto), which belonged to Japan until 1945, when it was appropriated by Russia.

Page 44   **Abe Toranosuke**
Full name, Abe Toranosuke Nobutaka. He succeeded as lord of Okabe in 1828, while still a young man, and retired (or died) around 1864.

Page 50   **like the rabbit did to the badger**
A reference to one of the best-known folktales in Japanese: *Kachi-kachi yama*, in which a rabbit revenges itself on a badger for killing an old lady (wife of the old man who is the rabbit's friend).

Notes on "John Manjirō"

Intro. **Roosevelt wrote a letter**
Nakahama Akira, Manjirō's grandson, quotes this letter in full in his *Nakahama Manjirō no shōgai* (Nakahama Manjirō's Life).

Chap. 1 **Denzō**
At this point his name was actually Fudenojō. Later on, in Hawaii, he changed it to Denzō for easier pronunciation.

Goemon
Goemon was actually Denzō's youngest brother. Ibuse was aware of this when he wrote the story, but preferred a father–son relationship for literary reasons.

the fifth day of the First Month
This is the first month of the old lunar calendar, actually January 27, 1841. Strictly speaking, two calendars should be used in the story: the lunar for events that take place in Japan, and the Western solar style for those that take place abroad. We have followed the lunar system until the castaways' first arrival in Hawaii, and the Western calendar thereafter, switching back to lunar after Manjirō's return to Japan. Since Ibuse uses the two calendars somewhat indiscriminately (and the Japanese government adopted the Western system in 1873), we use the Western calendar throughout the rest of the story, converting major recorded dates from the lunar count.

"stretching rope"
A fishing technique that involves one main line with a number of shorter, hooked and baited extensions attached to it.

Cape Yaso
A cape near the village of Okitsu.

Chap. 2 **The island**
The name of this island, appropriately enough, is Torishima or "Island of Birds" and lies southeast of the main islands of Japan.

148

Mountain of Swords
Tsurugi no yama (or *kenzan*). A well-known scene in Buddhist pictures of Hell is a dense throng of swords, "planted" in the ground and pointing upward to punish sinners who will be thrown on their tips.

Yamajū
This character, consisting of a "roof" and the number "ten," was one of the typical shop signs of the Edo period.

Chap. 3 **Sandwich archipelago**
When the Hawaiian Islands were first discovered, they were named after the Earl of Sandwich (who is also credited with the invention of the food).

Dr. George
Real name, Dr. Judd, a medical missionary who, although not the governor (a Hawaiian, Kekuanaoa, held that office), was a good friend to the castaways.

S. C. Damon
Reverend Samuel Chenery Damon, chaplain of a "Seamen's Bethel" and editor of *The Friend*. He followed Manjirō's career closely over the years and was often of assistance to him. But according to Warinner's book on Manjirō, *Voyager to Destiny*, Captain Whitfield himself put the question to Denzō, and Manjirō met Damon for the first time on his second visit to Hawaii, in 1848.

Chap. 4 **"John Man"**
Ibuse writes this with the first character of Manjirō, *man* ("ten thousand"), but in English the man himself spelled his name "John Mung" (a fair enough rendering of the Japanese pronunciation) or occasionally "Mungero."

Kingsmill Islands
Part of what are now known as the Gilbert Islands. As with many Pacific islands, they are famous for the battles fought there, on Tarawa in particular.

Eimeo
One of the Society Islands, where Tahiti is located.

Fairhaven
A town across the river from New Bedford, close enough for the towns to be known together sometimes as Fairhaven–New Bedford.

James Allen

The cooper Manjirō was apprenticed to seems to have been named Hussey, but it was a Miss Jane Allen who ran the school.

a mathematician by the name of Bartlett
Bartlett was in fact the headmaster of a large school, Bartlett's Academy, which offered advance courses.

São Tiago in the Cape Verde Islands
Ibuse gives this as Santiago in the Cape Heart (or Hart?) Archipelago. There are Santiagos in the Canaries and on Fernando Po, but since Warinner mentions a visit to Cape Verde, this location (actually an island) seemed most likely.

Doron group
We could not locate this place. There is a Dororian in the Philippines and an Indonesian Doro, but the islands north of Borneo are called the Spratlies.

Sentei
Japan, like many countries before the modern period of easy transportation (and even nowadays), had a multitude of regional dialects. Manjirō's style of language would not have been used much beyond his native Tosa.

Florida
Ibuse gives the name of this ship as "*Rororede*" and its captain's name as "*Kōkan*." He is trying to give a sense of the strangeness of foreign names to the castaways' ears, and to suggest the weird spelling of foreign names in older Japanese chronicles.

Chap. 5 ### king of the islands
This was Kamehameha II, successor to Kamehameha the Great. Warinner says it was the governor, Kekuanaoa, who took a special interest in the castaways.

Matsumae
Near the southern tip of Hokkaidō (or Ezo, as it was then called) by the Tsugaru Straits. There were few Japanese settlers on it at that time.

Maeha
Our gazetteers did not list this place, but there is a Makaha near Honolulu, and Warinner mentions the village of "Makai."

Chap. 6 ### Mr. Miller, the first officer
Nakahama Akira, Manjirō's grandson, gives the name Isachar Akin as

first officer of the *Franklin* in his *Nakahama Manjirō no shōgai*.

Batan Islands
This does not refer to the Bataan Peninsula, across the bay from Manila, but to the island group north of Luzon.

Captain Fitzmore
His real name was Whitmore, but Ibuse seems to have changed it to avoid confusion with Whitfield.

Mabunimagiri
A village on the southern tip of Okinawa.

Ogawa Shōnosuke
A junior official of the Satsuma clan, whose name does not appear in its registers.

high commissioner of Nagasaki
This was Lord Maki Yoshisada, governor of Shima.

Nishidamachi
A ward in the city of Kagoshima, in Kyūshū.

Lord Nariakira
Shimatsu Nariakira (1809–55), the progressive feudal lord of Satsuma (now Kagoshima Prefecture) in Kyūshū, favored the policy of opening the country to trade and foreign learning and welcomed the arrival of Perry's fleet at Uraga in 1853. He also encouraged shipbuilding.

report from the lord of Satsuma
Among other discrepancies, the report gives the date of the castaways' rescue as "about the third day of the Sixth Month," while Ibuse's narrative gives "on the seventh or eighth day of the Sixth Month." In actual fact, the log entry of the *John Howland* has "Sunday, June 27, 1841." It seems that Ibuse retains some inconsistencies to suggest the gap between memory and official record. Manjirō may also have concealed some of the facts from the officials, who had no knowledge of the outside world anyway.

the bridle-crested flag of Satsuma
Actually shaped like the old Japanese riding bit: a Greek cross in a circle.

Kinikakeoli
Probably a reference to Kekauluohi, the premier. Manjirō's confusion was understandable, for at this point Hawaii lay in the limbo between a sovereign kingdom and a U.S. colony. Officials of the monarchy had

republican titles and little power, representatives of America had modest titles but wide powers, and the traders and missionaries had no titles but a great deal of influence with both.

Christ's image
A test was devised near the end of Japan's "Christian century" (1543–1637) to force native converts to recant. It involved trampling (*efumi*) on a bronze image of Christ, a deadly insult in Japanese eyes. Many refused to do so, and died in agony.

Osome Hisamatsu
A popular romance about a doomed love affair ending in *shinjū* (double suicide).

Shigure no kotatsu, "The Hearth and the Rain"
A popular reworking of Chikamatsu's famous puppet play, *The Love Suicides at Amijima (Shinjū Ten no Amijima)*.

the lord of Satsuma
Shimatsu Nariakira, see note above.

Lord Matsudaira
Yamanouchi Yōdō (1827–72). The feudal lord of Manjirō's province, Tosa.

Chap. 8 ### Lord Abe Masahiro, the governor of Ise
Abe Masahiro (1819–57), senior councillor in the shogunate and clan leader of the Fukuyama domain in Bingo Province (now Hiroshima Prefecture). Although he did not personally favor the open-door policy, he was forced to conclude the treaties with Commodore Perry. The title "governor" (*kami*) had little practical meaning.

Egawa Tarōzaemon
See note for "A Geisha Remembers."

bateira
This comes from the Portuguese word for "boat." Modern Japanese includes many completely Japanized loanwords of this kind.

Ii Naosuke
Ii Naosuke (1815–60), lord of Ōmi (modern Shiga Prefecture), was an ardent advocate of opening the country. After becoming senior councillor, he suppressed opponents of this policy and was assassinated in 1860 by Satsuma clansmen.

Tōdō Takayuki

152

Feudal lord of the Anotsu clan of Ise (1814–95). Also called "lieuten-ant general of the left" and "governor of Izumi."

Hotta Masayoshi
Head of the Sakura clan (1810–64). As a member of the shōgun's cabinet (rōjū), he negotiated with Townsend Harris a proposed U.S.-Japan commercial treaty, but failed to conclude it.

Admiral Putyatin
Evfimii Vasilievich Putyatin (1803–83). He visited Japan a number of times. All the events pertaining to the Russian visit described in the story are historical facts.

Lord Shinmi of Buzen
Shinmi Masaoki (1822–69) served as gaikoku bugyō (commissioner for foreign countries) from 1859 to 1862.

Lord Muragaki of Awaji
Muragaki Norimasa (1813–80) also served as gaikoku bugyō from 1858 to 1863.

Powhatan
This had been one of Commodore Perry's ships on his Japan ex-pedition.

Lord Kimura of Settsu
Kimura Yoshitake (1830–1901) served as gunkan bugyō (commission-er for warships) from 1859 to 1863.

Katsu Rintarō
After studying "Dutch learning" and Western military science, Katsu (1823–99) embarked on a plan to build the shogunate a navy. After the Meiji Restoration, he became state councillor on naval affairs and a member of the Senate.

Fukuzawa Yukichi
A great Meiji scholar (1835–1901) who studied "Dutch learning" first, then English. After the official mission described in the story, he joined two more delegations to the West. He is best known for his intellec-tual contributions to the Japanese enlightenment. He founded Keiō, one of Japan's most famous universities, and his autobiography has been translated into English.

Kawamura
Kawamura Yūsen, author of The Secret History of California's Civiliza-tion, emigrated to Hawaii as a young woman and later moved on to

California, where she worked as a schoolteacher. Her book, published in 1930, gives a detailed account of the lives of early Japanese settlers in America.

mayor of San Francisco
San Francisco had no mayor at this point, but a board of supervisors, all of whom were present on this occasion. A man named Teschemacher was their president.

Captain Brooke
This was John Mercer Brooke, whose ship had been wrecked on the coast of Japan. He was taken back home on the *Kanrin maru* and incidentally served as a "consultant" to its untried crew.

Chap. 9 ### instructors of navigation
In 1857, the shogunate founded a school of navigation and naval drill called the Gunkan Sōrenjo. Hayashinami and Hayashi were its instructors.

Muraviev-Amurski
Nikolai Nikolaevich Muraviev-Amurski (1809–81), a Russian politician, was active in expanding Russia's eastern borders.

Aihun treaty
This treaty between Russia and China was completed in 1858. It recognized the main stem of the Amur River as the border between the two nations. Aihun was an open port in the northeastern region of the Amur.

Hung Hsiu-ch'üan
Hung Hsiu-ch'üan (1813–64), a native of Kuangtung Province, was the leader of the Taiping Rebellion, which rocked China and came close to toppling the dynasty. In 1850 he led an army of "God-worshipers" to victory and proclaimed Nanking the capital of "Heavenly Peace." Calling himself the "Heavenly King," he subdued sixteen provinces and ruled for almost fifteen years. Finally defeated by imperial forces, he committed suicide.

Sakhalin
The Japanese were aware of Russian designs on Karafuto (as they called Sakhalin) at a very early stage, but the fact that even Ezo (Hokkaidō) was sparsely populated made their claim on it weak. The Russo-Japanese War reestablished it, but the issue was not finally settled until 1945, when Stalin took it back.

Chōshū War

The Chōshū fief lay at the southern tip of Honshū. It first defied the shogunate in 1863, by firing upon foreign ships in the Straits of Shimonoseki. At first the Chōshū firebrands were brought to heel; then the government made the mistake of trying to suppress the clan entirely, with so little success that its weakness was made plain to other rebellious clans in Tosa and Satsuma.

Lord Oguri of Bungo
Oguri Tadamasa (1827–68) served as commissioner for foreign countries from 1860 to 1861.

Imozaki
A village on the shore of Tsushima Island, facing the Tsushima Straits (Nagasaki Prefecture).

Hirugaura
Another village further along the shore.

Hosokawa Junjirō
A famous scholar of law and political science (1834–1923).

Mitsukuri Rinshō
A prominent lawyer and legal scholar (1846–97).

Ōtori Keisuke
A personal retainer of the shōgun, who revolted against the government with Enomoto Buyō, but later joined its ranks and became well known as a diplomat (1832–1911).

Kaisei School
A predecessor of Tōkyō University, established in the last years of the shogunate by scholars of Western languages and scientific disciplines.

Ōyama Iwao
Field marshal of the Japanese army (1842–1916); excelled as a commander in both the Sino-Japanese and Russo-Japanese wars.

Yanaka, in Tokyo
Present-day Taitō Ward, northwest of Ueno Park.

Ibuse's Historical Fiction

1930–38	*Sazanami gunki*	"Waves: A War Diary"
1930	*Oranda dembō kimmizu*	"The Café from Holland"
1934	*Aokejima taigaiki*	"A General Account of Aokejima"
1937	*Sujō gimmi*	"The Family Tree Investigation"
1937	*John Manjirō hyōryūki*	"John Manjirō: A Castaway's Chronicle"
1938	*Biwazuka*	"The Biwa Mound"
1938	*Yujima fūzoku*	"The Mores of Yujima"
1939	*Yama o mite rōjin no kataru*	"An Old Man's Mountain Tale"
1939	*O-hori ni kansuru hanashi*	"The Story of the Moat"
1940	*Kawai sōdō*	"The Kawai Riot"
1940	*Enshin no gyōjō*	"Mementos of a Robber"
1943	*Fukigoe no shiro*	"The Castle of Fukigoe"
1946	*Futatsu no hanashi*	"Two Tales"
1946	*Wabisuke*	"Isle-on-the-Billows"
1949	*Toramatsu nisshi*	"The Toramatsu Journal"
1950	*Oshima no zonnengaki*	"A Geisha Remembers"
1952	*Yakushidōmae*	"In Front of the Inner Shrine of Yakushi"
1953	*Karusan yashiki*	The Karusan Mansion
1953–54	*Azuchi seminario*	"The Seminary of Azuchi"
1953	*Noheji no Mutsugorō ryakuden*	"The Life of Noheji Mutsugorō"
1954–55	*Hyōmin Usaburō*	Usaburō the Drifter
1955	*Kappa sōdō*	"The Water Imp Riot"
1955	*Kaikon mura no Yosaku*	"Yosaku the Settler"
1961	*Bushū hachigatajō*	"The Castle of Hachigata in Bushū"

Ibuse's Works Available in English Translation

Hakuchō no uta. "Swan Song." Tr. by G. W. Sargent. *Eigo Seinen*, v. 102, nos. 9–12, 1956.

Henrō yado. "Pilgrims' Inn." Tr. by John Bester. *Lieutenant Lookeast, and Other Stories.* Tokyo, Kodansha International, 1971; London, Secker and Warburg, 1971. Pp. 53–58.

Honjitsu kyūshin. "No Consultation Today." Tr. by Edward Seidensticker. *Japan Quarterly,* v. 8, no. 1, 1961. Pp. 50–79. *No Consultation Today.* Tokyo, Hara Shobō, 1964. Pp. 8–123.

John Manjirō hyōryūki. "John Manjiro, the Cast-away." Tr. by Hisakazu Kaneko. Tokyo, Hokuseido, 1940.

Kaikon mura no Yosaku. "Yosaku, the Settler." Tr. by John Bester. *Lieutenant Lookeast, and Other Stories.* Tokyo, Kodansha International, 1971; London, Secker and Warburg, 1971. Pp. 113–29.

Kakitsubata. "The Crazy Iris." Tr. by Ivan Morris. *Encounter,* v. 6, no. 5, 1956. Pp. 92–93.

Kan'ya. "A Cold Night." Tr. by George Saito. *Japan P. E. N. News,* no. 18, March 1966. Pp. 1–6.

Kappa sōdō. "Catching a Kappa, or Water Imp." Tr. by Kiyoaki Nakao. *Two Stories by Masuji Ibuse.* Tokyo, Hokuseido, 1970. Pp. 4–28.

Koi. "Carp." Tr. by John Bester. *Lieutenant Lookeast, and Other Stories.* Tokyo, Kodansha International, 1971; London, Secker and Warburg, 1971. Pp. 91–95.

Kuroi ame. *Black Rain.* Tr. by John Bester. *Japan Quarterly,* v. 14, nos. 2–4, 1967; v. 15, nos. 1–3, 1968.

Black Rain. Tr. by John Bester. Tokyo, Kodansha International, 1969; London, Secker and Warburg, 1971.

Noheji no Mutsugorō ryakuden. "The Life of Mutsugoro of Noheji." Tr. by Kiyoaki Nakao. *Two Stories by Masuji Ibuse.* Tokyo, Hokuseidō, 1970. Pp. 32–72.

Noriai jidōsha. "The Charcoal Bus." Tr. by Ivan Morris. *Modern Japanese Stories,* ed. by I. Morris. London, Spottiswoode, 1961; Tokyo, Tuttle, 1962. Pp. 212–22.

Sanshōuo. "The Salamander." Tr. by Tadao Katayama. *The Reeds,* v. 2, 1956. Pp. 51–64.

"The Salamander." Tr. by Leon Zolbrod. *The East,* v. 1, no. 2, 1964. Pp. 21–23.

"Salamander." Tr. by Sadamichi Yokoo and Sanford Goldstein. *Japan Quarterly,* v. 13, no. 1, 1966. Pp. 71–75.

"Salamander." Tr. by John Bester. *Lieutenant Lookeast, and Other Stories.* Tokyo, Kodansha International, 1971; London, Secker and Warburg, 1971. Pp. 59–65.

Tajinko mura. "Tajinko Village." Tr. by John Bester. *Lieutenant Lookeast, and Other Stories.* Tokyo, Kodansha International, 1971; London, Secker and Warburg, 1971. Pp. 135–247.

Tange shi tei. "At Mr. Tange's." Tr. by Sadamichi Yokoo and Sanford Goldstein. *Literature East and West,* v. 13, nos. 1–2, 1969. Pp. 167–81.

"Life at Mr. Tange's." Tr. by John Bester. *Lieutenant Lookeast, and Other Stories.* Tokyo, Kodansha International, 1971; London, Secker and Warburg, 1971. Pp. 97–111.

Ushitora jiisan. "Old Ushitora." Tr. by John Bester. *Lieutenant Lookeast, and Other Stories.* Tokyo, Kodansha International, 1971; London, Secker and Warburg, 1971. Pp. 67–89.

Yane no ue no sawan. "Sawan on the Roof." Tr. by Yokichi Miyamoto with Frederic Will. *Chicago Review,* v. 19, no. 1, 1966. Pp. 51–54.

"Sawan on the Rooftop." Tr. by Tadao Katayama. *The Reeds,* v. 11, 1967. Pp. 127–34.

"Savan on the Roof." Tr. by John Bester. *Lieutenant Lookeast, and Other Stories.* Tokyo, Kodansha International, 1971; London, Secker and Warburg, 1971. Pp. 129–34.

Yofuke to ume no hana. "Plum Blossom by Night." Tr. by John Bester. *Lieutenant Lookeast, and Other Stories.* Tokyo, Kodansha International, 1971; London, Secker and Warburg, 1971. Pp. 11–22.

Yōhai taichō. "A Far-worshipping Commander." Tr. by Glenn Shaw. *Japan Quarterly,* v. 1, no. 1, 1954. Pp. 53–73. *No Consultation Today.* Tokyo, Hara Shobō, 1964. Pp. 126–213.

"The Far-worshipping Commander." Tr. by Glenn Shaw. *The Shadow of Sunrise,* ed. by Shoichi Saeki. Tokyo, Kodansha International, 1966; London, Ward Lock, 1966. Pp. 157–86.

"Lieutenant Lookeast." Tr. by John Bester. *Lieutenant Lookeast, and Other*

Stories. Tokyo, Kodansha International, 1971; London, Secker and Warburg, 1971. Pp. 23–51.

Bibliography

Lifton, R., "Black Rain," *Death in Life* (1967), pp. 543–55.

Kimball, A., "After the Bomb," *Crisis in Identity and Contemporary Japanese Novels* (1973), pp. 43–59.

Liman, A. V., "Ibuse's Black Rain," in Tsuruta, K., and Swann, T., eds., *Approaches to the Modern Japanese Novel* (1976), pp. 45–72.

Liman, A. V., "Carp," "Pilgrim's Inn," in Swann, T., and Tsuruta, K., eds., *Approaches to the Modern Japanese Short Story* (1982), pp. 83–101.

DISCOVER JAPAN, VOLS. 1 AND 2
Words, Customs, and Concepts

The Japan Culture Institute

Essays and photographs illuminate 200 ideas and customs of Japan.

THE UNFETTERED MIND
Writings of the Zen Master to the Sword Master

Takuan Sōhō / Translated by William Scott Wilson

Philosophy as useful to today's corporate warriors as it was to seventeenth century samurai.

THE JAPANESE THROUGH AMERICAN EYES

Sheila K. Johnson

"Cogent...as skeptical of James Clavell's *Shogun* as it is of William Ouchi's *Theory Z*."—*Publisher's Weekly*

Available only in Japan.

BEYOND NATIONAL BORDERS
Reflections on Japan and the World

Kenichi Ohmae

"[Ohmae is Japan's] only management guru."—*Financial Times*

Available only in Japan.

THE COMPACT CULTURE
The Japanese Tradition of "Smaller is Better"

O-Young Lee / Translated by Robert N. Huey

A long history of skillfully reducing things and concepts to their essentials reveals the essence of the Japanese character and, in part, accounts for Japan's business success.

THE HIDDEN ORDER
Tokyo through the Twentieth Century

Yoshinobu Ashihara

"Mr. Ashihara shows how, without anybody planning it, Japanese architecture has come to express the vitality of Japanese life."
—*Daniel J. Boorstin*
